Had her stalker followed her earlier out to O'Reilly Manor to threaten her... or worse?

Lily didn't relax until she parked her car alongside her house. When James pulled in behind her, she waved him off.

"I want to make sure everything's secure," he told her as he got out.

"Since when did you become a safety expert?"

He waved a hand down his dress uniform. He took a step closer, hovering over her. She resisted the urge to reach up and place her palm on his chest—to keep him away or to bring him closer, she wasn't sure. "I know how to protect you," he said.

The memory of James training a gun on the thug replayed in her mind. "I hate to admit it, but I'm still rattled."

"You need to be careful." The concern in his voice settled on her shoulders like a cozy shawl. It had been a long time since someone looked after her.

"I have never felt threatened living here," she said. *Until tonight.*

Books by Alison Stone

Love Inspired Suspense

Plain Pursuit
Critical Diagnosis

ALISON STONE

left snowy Buffalo, New York, and headed a thousand miles south to earn an industrial engineering degree at Georgia Tech in Hotlanta. Go Yellow Jackets! She loved the South, but true love brought her back north.

After the birth of her second child, Alison left corporate America for full-time motherhood. She credits an advertisement to write children's books for sparking her interest in writing. She never did complete a children's book, but she did have success writing articles for local publications before finding her true calling, writing romantic suspense.

Alison lives with her husband of more than twenty years and their four children in western New York, where the summers are absolutely gorgeous and the winters are perfect for curling up with a good book—or writing one.

Besides writing, Alison keeps busy volunteering at her children's schools, driving her girls to dance and watching her boys race motocross.

Alison loves to hear from her readers at Alison@AlisonStone.com. For more information please visit her website, www.AlisonStone.com. She's also chatty on Twitter, @Alison_Stone.

CRITICAL DIAGNOSIS

ALISON STONE

HARLEQUIN® LOVE INSPIRED® SUSPENSE

ISBN-13: 978-0-373-67620-0

CRITICAL DIAGNOSIS

This edition published by arrangement with Love Inspired Books.

www.Harlequin.com

Printed in U.S.A.

Trust in the Lord with all your heart;
do not depend on your own understanding.
Seek his will in all you do, and he will
show you which path to take.

—*Proverbs* 3:5–6

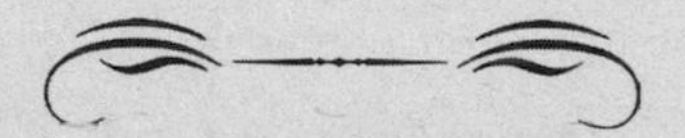

To my oldest, Scotty.
Congratulations on your high school graduation.
I don't know where the past eighteen years have gone,
but I loved every minute of watching you grow into
the fine young man you are today. God bless you
in all you do as you move on to the next phase
of your life. Follow your dreams,
work hard and success will follow.

To my husband, Scott,
and the rest of the gang, Alex, Kelsey and Leah.
You guys are the reason I work so hard.
Love you always and forever.

To my beautiful niece, Lily.
The smartest four-year-old I know.
I named the heroine in *Critical Diagnosis* after you.
I'll save a copy for you to read when you get a
little older. Sorry, there's no princess in this book,
but it's still a really good story. I promise.

To Rachel Dylan,
a fellow Harlequin Love Inspired Suspense author,
who read an earlier version of this book and gave
me some wonderful insight that made this
final version so much better. Thank you.

ONE

"Three Saturdays in a row." James rested his hip against the desk in the cramped nurses' station and met Lily's gaze. His close-cropped hair made him look every bit the army captain he was. "I appreciate it. The patients appreciate it. It seems more and more people are counting on this clinic." He tossed the medical chart on top of the pile, a satisfied smile on his handsome face. A day well spent. The chart teetered. Lily lunged to grab it. James did the same, his solid hand brushing against hers, but he was faster.

"Oh, boy " Lily McAllister dipped her head and tucked a strand of hair behind her ear. "I don't want to be around if those charts hit the floor and all the files scatter." She stood and divided the pile in two, stacking them neatly next to one another. Stepping back, she planted her fists squarely on her hips. "There."

James laughed, his white smile bright against his tanned skin. "Nancy would have my head on

Monday. She already gives me a tongue-lashing when I file the charts. Apparently, I'm messing with her system. I guess it takes more than a month for the new guy to figure out *the system.* Even though I was the one who set up the system before I enlisted in the army. Go figure."

Lily lifted her palms in an *I-totally-had-nothing-to-do-with-it-if-the-files-get-messed-up* gesture. "I'm just the weekend help." She scooted out from the confined space and leaned her elbows on the counter. "It feels fantastic to escape the research lab and actually practice medicine. It's been a long time."

"I appreciate the help." He lifted his eyebrows and bestowed his best persuasive smile on her. She had seen it before. "You on for next Saturday, too?" The free health-care clinic was obviously short on staff. While the man running it was obviously short on tact.

Mirroring his raised eyebrows, Lily slid off her stethoscope and slipped it into her bag. "I'm beginning to think you're taking advantage of my good nature."

A mischievous glint lit his eyes. "Never. Think of the fine people of Orchard Gardens who count on this clinic." He leaned in closer. "Who count on you."

"Captain James O'Reilly, is this how it works in the army? You say 'jump' and people ask how high?" She rested her chin on the heel of her hand.

"I'm not in the army now, am I?" He winked. "How about it? Next Saturday? Call it a date?"

Collapsing her arms on the counter, she dropped her forehead onto her arm. Lifting her gaze, she found him watching her. "Well," she said with an air of being put upon, "since you asked so nicely." A flicker of a smile teased the corners of her lips. She'd fail miserably as an actress. Good thing she had succeeded beyond her wildest hopes as a researcher. Regen, her research, was currently in clinical trials. She could finally breathe. She was this close to getting a treatment on the market for the disease that had killed her mother and afflicted her niece. It had been the culmination of years of hard work and the answer to a zillion prayers muttered into her wet, tearstained pillow. So it only felt right to give back to the small community where she had been afforded so much.

Lily tapped the counter with the palm of her hand. "I'll make sure all the medicine cabinets in back are locked. You got the front doors?" They both had to be at James's grandfather's eightieth birthday party in a couple hours.

"Sure." The single word came out clipped, as if he were biting back further comment.

Lily strode down the long corridor of Orchard

Gardens Clinic. Once a stately Victorian, it had been converted into a medical practice by James's parents, both physicians, when James was still learning how to color between the lines on the pages of his Bible-themed coloring book.

James had returned home to carry on the tradition after serving as a physician in the U.S. Army for the past several years. She wondered how long he'd have time for the clinic, considering the rampant rumors floating around town. Apparently, James was slotted to head Medlink, the pharmaceutical company his grandfather had founded. Many speculated the elder O'Reilly's health was deteriorating.

The small town was short on physicians, but not on rumors.

She pushed open the last door on the right. The high-pitched creak and the chill from the air pumping out of the AC unit perched in the window made her skin prickle. Hurrying her pace, she secured the drug cabinets, turned off the printer and the AC. Her ears buzzed with deafening silence.

A banana peel in the garbage caught her eye. Unsure the janitor was scheduled over the weekend, she decided to tug out the liner and toss it into the Dumpster. If she didn't, come Monday morning, a ripe banana would be a nasty surprise.

Voices reached her from the front of the clinic.

A last-minute patient must have come in. She angled her head and noticed Mrs. Benson, who had been in earlier with her two-year-old granddaughter, Chloe, due to an ear infection. Perhaps the sweet child hadn't settled down quickly enough for the elderly woman. Not wanting to disturb them, Lily headed toward the solid-steel door retrofitted for the building's second life.

The clock marked the hour with a soft chime. Six o'clock. Butterflies flitted in her stomach. Dr. Declan O'Reilly was due to arrive at the party at eight. That meant she had to arrive before then or risk ruining the surprise—and Mrs. O'Reilly's wrath. She hustled down the short flight of stairs. She twisted the thumb turn, releasing the dead bolt. The back door opened onto a small parking lot. For the briefest of moments, she tilted her face and basked in the warm summer sun.

She'd be locked out if she let the door slam. A broom rested against the back wall, a perfect wedge. She set it in place and then headed toward the Dumpster in the far corner of the lot.

A tall row of evergreens separated the clinic's property from a squat row of brick apartment buildings. A car sped past on the country road out front, the boom-boom-boom from its car speakers vibrating through her.

Clamping her mouth shut, she grabbed the

small, black door on the Dumpster with the tips of her fingers and pulled. The door slid in fits and starts, getting hung up in its tracks. *Ugh.* Flies and an acrid smell hovered over the steaming pile of trash. Her lungs screamed for fresh air. She tossed the bag inside. It landed with a squishy thud.

The deep hum of an engine idling near the apartments seeped into her consciousness. Backing away from the rancid Dumpster, she drew in a breath and peered through the branches. A beat-up, lime-green car with one of those do-it-yourself paint jobs was parked on the other side. Her pulse whoosh-whooshed in her ears, as if God whispered a warning.

Get back inside, where it's safe.

Yet she dismissed her paranoia. The small town of Orchard Gardens was one of the safest towns in America to live. It said so on the quaint sign on the main road into town.

Yet instinct urged her on. She spun on her heel and hustled toward the back door of the clinic. The trees rustled and solid steps sounded on the hard earth behind her. Her gaze darted toward the tree line. Heat swept up her neck, her cheeks. A man, his baseball cap slung low on his forehead, strode toward her. The menacing expression on his hardened features annihilated any doubts. He was coming toward her.

Her vision narrowed.

Move faster.

Get inside.

Slam the door.

The words echoed over and over in her mind. The gravel at the edge of the parking lot crunched under his determined footsteps. Lily sprinted the remaining fifteen feet to the door. She didn't care if she mistook his intentions. Better safe than sorry. She wouldn't let him get inside the clinic. The news was saturated with pharmacies and clinics targeted by drug-crazed thugs.

Dear Lord, help me.

Without enough time to get inside and secure the door, she grabbed the broom and pushed her hip against it. The steel door slammed shut—locked—with an air of finality. A flush of tingles blanketed her scalp. Sweaty palms compromised her death grip on the broom handle. Determined not to be a victim, she braced her feet, squaring off with the thug. Her gaze shot to the side of the green clapboard house. She'd never make it around front. The wall of evergreens mocked her. The man bore down on her, his mouth curved into a sardonic grin.

Privacy was a double-edged sword.

Bracing herself against the door, she hiked her chin. "Hey," she said, her commanding tone at odds with the knots twisting her insides. "What do you want? The clinic's closed." She adjusted her hands on the broom, trying to get a better grip. White dots danced in her vision, her system flooding with adrenaline.

The stocky man had dark, beady eyes under the visor of a Buffalo Bills cap. Scruffy whiskers grew in uneven patches on his jaw. Reaching around her, he yanked on the door handle. It didn't budge. He pounded his fist on the door right over her head. She startled. His hat slanted back, revealing an unfamiliar symbol drawn with thick marker on the bill's underside. He quickly pulled the hat down, shading his eyes.

"Why'd ya do that for? Stupid lady." He narrowed his gaze. His skin was pocked with acne and his eyes flashed dark. Tufts of dirty-blond hair poked out from under his cap. He glowered, intimidating her. His stale breath mingled with hers. Beer and tobacco made her nauseous with their stench.

"Clinic's closed." She tried her calm approach again, fully aware he wasn't here for medical care. He was here for prescription drugs. He had to be. He slammed his fist against the door a second time, inches from her head. She slid out from under his arm, holding solidly on to the handle of the broom.

Come on, James. Come on, James. He had to have heard the pounding.

The thug cursed at her with a gruff voice. He stalked toward her; his menacing expression made her chest ache and she gasped for a breath. He raised his arm again and this time Lily mustered courage she didn't know she had. She hoisted the broom and slammed it down against his forearm. The wood splintered.

His bold laugh vibrated through her, frying her frayed nerves. He snatched the broom from her hands and tossed it aside. Seizing her shoulder, he shoved her down, her knee taking the brunt of her weight. A sharp pain exploded through her kneecap.

"You shouldn't have done that." He kicked the loose gravel, the tiny pebbles assaulting her bare arms. Looking up, she squinted against the sunlight. The taut muscles in the thug's jaw spoke of his restraint.

Please, dear Lord, protect me.

"Don't hurt me. I'm a doctor here at the clinic." She scrunched her eyes shut against another onslaught of gravel. She pulled her legs in and maneuvered around. Slowly. "I'm going to sit here." She lifted her hands in a nonthreatening gesture. "You don't have to hurt me."

"You think that gives you a pass? Just because you're a *doc*-tor?" Spittle flew from his lips. The deranged look in his eyes sent fear coursing through her, making her limbs tremble. "Maybe I score extra points if I get me a *lady doc*-tor?"

Her mind raced. "Please, you don't have to do this. You haven't done anything you can't undo. Please." Leaning against the side of the house, she pushed to a standing position. He seemed too agitated to notice.

The back door burst open, catching Lily's ankle. The thug growled at her, scrabbled backward, his arms pinwheeling before he crashed to the ground. With amazing agility, he sprang to his feet and reached behind him at his waist.

Lily's throat tightened.

"Stop!" James roared, training a gun on the thug. The man's mouth flattened; something flickered across his flinty eyes only she could see. Indecision? Recognition? Defeat?

The attacker seemed to hesitate a fraction before spinning around and jackrabbiting out of there, escaping through the evergreens. A loud muffler fired up and a vehicle tore away from the apartment parking lot. Closing her eyes, Lily breathed a sigh of relief and fell against the house.

James tucked the gun into his waistband.

Lily lifted a shaky hand. "You have a gun…." It seemed a ridiculous thing to say; he was in the army, but still. She hadn't expected him to have it at the clinic. Her teeth chattered.

What if he hadn't?

"Are you okay?" He gripped her forearm possessively.

She blinked against the grit scraping against her eyelids. Discreetly, she tested her weight on her knee, careful to keep her expression neutral. "Fine," she bit out. "Just a little banged up."

James eased his grip and gently ran his thumb down her arm, deep concern radiating from his kind brown eyes. "He got away so fast, I didn't get a good look at him. He had his hat tugged down. What happened? What did he do to you?"

"I…I think he wanted drugs. From the clinic." She licked her parched lips. "He never said. When I tried to stop him, he threw me on the ground. But I'm fine. Really." Sidestepping his touch, she brushed her khakis. Her violent fall had torn a hole at the knee. She was going to be sore tomorrow, that was for sure.

A muscle twitched in his jaw. "Tell me what happened."

"He came from there." She pointed at the trees. Reality was settling in behind her eyes, pulsing, throbbing, aching. "I had the back door propped open so I could take out the trash. But I got it closed just in time."

James ran a hand over her shoulder. "Why

would you slam the door shut?" A line creased his forehead.

"I was afraid of what would happen if he got inside. I saw you with Mrs. Benson and her granddaughter. I was afraid of what he might do." Her knees bent, then straightened. "I've heard so many stories of crazed druggies...." The memory of the thug's sour breath made her nauseous. Blinking, she inhaled deeply, filling her lungs with the smell of summer and clean. James always smelled so clean.

"My only thought was to keep him outside. Away from the clinic," she said.

He smoothed her hair and tucked a strand behind her ear. "You should have never tried to take him on yourself."

Lowering her gaze, she bit her bottom lip. A new feeling, one she didn't want to acknowledge, softened the shield around her heart.

He leaned back to look at the hole in her pant leg. "Let's go inside so I can take a look at your knee." Unexpected embarrassment heated her cheeks at the thought of James tending her injury. She had been so stupid. She should have never gone out back by herself. Even though they were in Orchard Gardens, she knew the buddy system was safer. She had heard the horror stories on the news about thugs and their desperate drug addictions.

Drugs didn't care about zip codes.

Shaking her head, Lily held up her hands. "I'm fine, really." She took a few steps, stifling a grimace. "See? Perfectly fine."

He eyed her skeptically. "Let's call the police."

He unlocked the door and guided her inside with a hand to the small of her back.

Lily glanced up at him. "I'm sorry. Now we're going to be late for your grandfather's birthday party."

James waved his hand in dismissal. "I'll deal with him. He'll understand." He leaned in close, his breath whispering across her cheek. "I can't let anything happen to his star researcher."

TWO

James weaved through the crowd gathered at O'Reilly Manor, his grandmother's gauche name for her oversize home sitting on the escarpment overlooking the town of Orchard Gardens, New York. Every single person associated with Medlink Pharmaceutical, his grandfather's company and the largest employer for sixty miles, had to be crammed into this room. It didn't take long before James spotted Lily standing in the corner, her long brown hair loose around her bare shoulders.

Lily looked up, their eyes connected, and a smile touched her pink lips.

James made his way over to her. "You look…" He searched for the right word.

"Like I'd rather be somewhere else?" She tilted her head, a sparkle in her brown eyes.

"I was going to say 'beautiful.'"

Her fingers fluttered at the hollow of her neck. "This cocktail dress is a far cry from my lab coat."

"The color suits you." He glanced down. A hint of a bandage poked out from under the hem of the lavender dress. The bandage he had secured around her scraped knee. "Are you okay?"

"I'll feel better once I identify the guy who attacked me. I wish I didn't have to wait until Monday morning to check out the photo array Chief Farley's putting together. I can't believe he thinks gangs from Buffalo are targeting small towns." She shifted her weight and sighed. "I'm grateful the police chief was able to make it to the clinic so quickly even though he didn't have the most reassuring news."

"We're old friends. We went to high school together."

"Really? I didn't see him as a wearing-a-suit-coat-with-a-crest kind of guy."

"Oh, he isn't." James took a step closer to avoid getting bumped by the waiter carrying some kind of hors d'oeuvre wrapped in bacon. His stomach rumbled. "I went to public school for the first two years of high school." The words *while my parents were alive* got caught in his throat.

"I had no idea.... Public school." She said the words as though she was trying them on for size.

"My grandparents forced me to go to boarding school for the last two years." He tried to keep the derision out of his tone, but realized he failed miserably.

A hand brushed his shoulder. "And we were such horrible grandparents." His grandmother hooked her hand around his elbow and leaned toward Lily. "You'd think his grandfather and I were sending him off to the state penitentiary, he put up such a fuss."

"I didn't see you there, Grandmother." James patted her hand. "Wonderful party for Grandfather."

"I'm a foolish old lady for throwing a surprise party for an eighty-year-old man with a heart condition." His grandmother lifted her hand and wiggled her fingers at a guest walking nearby.

"My grandfather's a tough old coot." James forced a laugh.

His grandmother shook her head in disapproval. "That tough old coot is ready to slow down and travel with me. We're both glad you're home. Six years was far too long to give to the army."

James bit back a retort. Serving as a physician in the army had been fulfilling, far more than being a suit at a corporate job ever would. He cut his gaze toward Lily. The smile had slipped from her face.

"I'm glad to see you two together." His grandmother glanced over her shoulder at the guests milling around her home, her attention already waning. "It gives me hope. I so dearly want great-grandbabies."

Next to him, Lily covered her mouth with her napkin and coughed.

"I need to go. I don't want to be rude to my guests." And with that, his grandmother strolled away.

"Elinor's always been something else," Lily said, coughing a few more times.

"Don't mind her. She likes to assert her authority in all things." James gently touched the small of Lily's back. "Let's step outside and get some fresh air."

They stepped through the French doors to a deserted patio. "Finally, peace and quiet."

A faraway look descended into Lily's eyes as she gazed toward the twinkling lights surrounding the pool area. "The first time I walked into O'Reilly Manor, I think I was eight. My mother had just gotten this great new job as a housekeeper for some really rich people who lived on the escarpment. Neither one of us had ever been in a house this big."

"My grandmother definitely likes showy things."

"I loved this yard." Lily took a few tentative steps and traced a groove in the top of the low stone wall. "I couldn't figure out why someone didn't put a tire swing on the beautiful oak tree out back. You know, the one next to the carriage house."

James smiled at her. "I guess I never thought about it. Growing up, I was hardly here. Explains why we never met until you were much older. I traveled with my parents as they did missionary work and brought health care to the underserved around the world."

Lily seemed to smile to herself. "It makes sense that you decided to be a physician in the army."

"Yes, I wanted to honor my parents' memory."

"How are you, dear cousin?" James's cousin, Stephanie, stepped out onto the patio and disturbed the tranquil mood. She hoisted her wineglass in a pseudo toast, seeming to regard him for a moment much like an alpha dog determined to protect its territory.

"I figured you'd be in there schmoozing with the investors since you're the new head of Medlink."

"Grandfather's still running the show, last I checked." James didn't bother to hide his amusement. He and his cousin, the only grandchildren, shared a siblinglike rivalry—and a lopsided one at that. James had always been the favored grandchild, such as it was.

Stephanie waved her hand in dismissal. "That's

simply a formality." She pursed her lips and shook her head. "The old glass ceiling still applies even when it comes to family." Stephanie took a quick breath and continued, "Can you believe this, Lily? Dr. James O'Reilly here is gone for *years* and—" Stephanie snapped her fingers "—just like that, he's back and Grandfather passes the baton. I don't—"

James caught his cousin's hand midgesture. Stephanie narrowed her gaze. Her mouth froze with an unspoken word on her lips.

"Don't ruin the party by discussing business," James said, releasing his cousin's hand.

Lily wandered a few feet away to put her empty glass on a serving tray and perhaps to distance herself from the mounting tension.

"I wouldn't dream of it." Stephanie's eyes grew hard. Her gaze shifted and she seemed to zero in on Lily's feet. "Dear," she called, "you seem to be limping a bit. Is something wrong?"

James's gaze locked with Lily's, silently imploring her to not bring up the disturbance at the clinic. If Stephanie knew, she might mention it to their grandparents, spoiling their evening.

Lily lifted her foot and brushed her fingers across the strap of her shoe. "My shoes are killing me," she said without missing a beat.

Stephanie tipped her head toward the pool.

"Why don't you soak them in the hot tub? No one would be the wiser."

"That sounds like a wonderful idea."

Stephanie lifted her hands, her polished nails dark against her fair skin. "Go for it." She nodded at James. "I better mingle." She turned and strolled inside. Her red gown popped in a sea of muted colors. Slowing by a group of male partygoers, she made a comment and tossed her long blond hair over her shoulder. They all laughed politely, probably hoping to attract her attention. Unfortunately for them, his cousin had her eye on only one thing: running Medlink.

James turned his attention back to Lily. "Stephanie's well suited for this. She really knows how to work a crowd." She'd have potential investors clamoring to take their money in the hopes of catching her eye.

"Why do you suppose your grandfather chose you over your cousin, then?"

James stared into her brown eyes. He made it a habit to never bash family, but he trusted Lily not to betray his confidence. "Stephanie may be an O'Reilly, but her mother is the black sheep of the family. My aunt Tiffany had Stephanie when she was only sixteen. My grandparents disowned their daughter."

Lily's eyes widened. "I had no idea."

"Stephanie had a rough upbringing. My grandparents only came back into Stephanie's life when it was time for college. Stephanie worked hard, went to graduate school and was welcomed back into the fold." He rubbed his brow. "But she always seems to be trying to prove she belongs." He caught a hint of Stephanie's red dress in the crowd. "Grandfather never made it easy. Stephanie looks just like her mother. It's a constant reminder."

Lily closed her eyes briefly, her long lashes sweeping against her cheeks. "Everyone has a skeleton in their closet."

James's gaze landed squarely on her. "Yes, they do."

Lily leaned on the stone wall and lifted her foot, tugging on the strap of her shoe. "Do you think Stephanie will give you a hard time when you take over as CEO?"

"I don't plan to take over as CEO."

Lily put her foot down and tilted her head. "What are you talking about?"

"I plan to reenlist, but wanted to wait until after my grandfather's celebration to tell my grandparents."

"But why not tell Stephanie? It's clearly making her miserable."

"Stephanie likes a challenge. If things were handed to her, she wouldn't appreciate it."

"Really?" Lily put some weight on her foot and grimaced. She obviously wasn't buying it.

"Maybe." A grin tugged at the corner of his mouth. "But it's more fun this way. I'm meeting with Grandfather and Stephanie on Monday. I'll put her out of her misery then. Stephanie will be so grateful, she'll be sure to continue funding the free health-care clinic."

"You can be persuasive."

"When it's something I want, yes."

Lily rolled her eyes. "I already agreed to work next Saturday at the clinic."

"I'm honored. I'm surprised you can make the time, considering how high profile your research has become." He paused a moment. "The *Garden Gazette* did a nice feature on you."

Lily sliced her hand through the air. "I hated doing that interview. It was your grandmother's idea."

"Anything to shine a bright spotlight on my grandfather. I'm sure my grandmother was thrilled when it came out this morning, the same day as Grandfather's birthday celebration."

"I don't like the attention." A soft breeze blew Lily's long brown hair back off her bare shoulders, releasing a flowery scent mixed with the chlorine from the pool. "I prefer staying in the lab or, when I get a chance, treating patients. I've never been comfortable on display."

"That surprises me. Someone as beautiful as you."

She eyed him skeptically. "Ah, you underestimated yourself. You can schmooze with the best of them."

He tilted his head to meet her gaze. "You should be proud. Your research stands to make Medlink a lot of money."

"That's secondary to finding a cure for the disease that killed my mother and now my poor niece…." Lily cleared her throat. "I'm determined to make sure Emily lives a long life." She brushed her fingers through her hair. Lily glanced toward the people socializing in his grandparents' great room. "The party's in full swing."

"Let's go wish my grandfather a happy birthday." He held out his elbow, but she didn't take it.

Lily pouted. "I don't think I can walk another step between my bruised knee and these killer shoes." She leaned on the wall again and slipped one shoe off, then the other. "I don't want to go traipsing through the party barefoot." She glanced toward the backyard. "I'm going to soak my feet in the hot tub for a few minutes. Maybe then I'll be able to slip on my shoes long enough to wish Dr. O'Reilly a happy birthday."

James frowned. The lights on the pool fence provided enough illumination to indicate the gate, but otherwise, the area was cast in heavy shadows. "I'll go with you, then."

Lily waved him off, dangling her fancy shoes in her hand. "No, you go ahead. I know where everything is. Remember, I lived in the carriage house off and on when I was going to college." She patted his chest. "Give me ten minutes."

"Okay, not a minute longer."

James watched Lily walk to the pool gate on tiptoes. She fumbled with the latch for a minute before finding the release. She gave him a quick wave and disappeared behind the hedges.

Lily strolled over to the control box on the wall and set the dial on the hot-tub timer for ten minutes. Just ten minutes and she'd rejoin the party. The stamped concrete felt warm on her bare toes. She dropped her shoulders and sighed. The mere thought of submerging her aching feet into the hot, bubbling water was delicious. She glanced toward the house. Only the second story of the stately home was visible over the perfectly manicured shrubs bordering the pool area.

The hot-tub jets roared to life. She set her shoes on top of a glass table nearby. A dim blue light glowed under the rolling water. Tugging her cocktail dress, she hiked it to just above her knees and sat by the step, careful not to dip the hem into the water. She examined her bandaged knee for a second before extending her legs into the tepid water.

She glanced back at the control panel. Maybe turning on the jets wasn't such a good idea. The gurgling water spit at her, leaving tiny dark dots on her lavender cocktail dress. But once she had her feet submerged, it would have taken a fork truck to move her. Leaning back, she braced her arms against the smooth concrete and closed her eyes. Ten minutes.

Just ten minutes.

Lily's thoughts drifted to when she'd first noticed James among the party guests. His strong profile, short cropped hair and dress army uniform would have made any woman proud to be escorted by him. But he hadn't arrived with anyone. She folded the hem of her dress and scooted back a fraction from the edge of the hot tub, distracting herself from thoughts of handsome James O'Reilly. Despite Elinor O'Reilly's musings, neither of them was in a position to settle down. He planned to reenlist. She never planned to marry. Work was her life. It had to be. Too much was at stake.

A rustling behind her made her bolt upright. She snapped her head in the direction of the noise, but didn't see anything amiss. Her heart jackhammered, a steady beat above the hum of the hot-tub jets. Her gaze ping-ponged around the pool area, trying to decipher the shadows. A few deck chairs. A table. A folded umbrella flapping in the breeze.

Tamping down her unease, she swooshed her feet in the water. But she couldn't relax. Grabbing on to the metal railing, she pulled herself to her feet and stepped out of the hot tub. She scooped up her shoes from the table and glared at them with contempt. She'd have to slip them on and suck it up for as long as it took to find Dr. O'Reilly, wish him well and make her excuses to call it a night.

Plopping down on the nearest lounge chair, she smoothed the hem of her dress and slipped her foot into her shoe. She was struggling with the delicate buckle when a clammy hand seized her shoulder. She froze and gasped. The distinct whiff of alcohol mixed with chlorine sent icy shards of fear shooting through her veins. Glancing up, she met the beady eyes of the man who had attacked her in the parking lot of the clinic.

She opened her mouth to scream, but he was quicker. He clamped his callused hand over her mouth. She bit back the urge to retch.

He forced a piece of paper into her hand. "I know who you are."

Lily struggled to catch a decent breath under his dirty hand, flattened against her lips.

"I can get to you whenever I want." He

jammed her upper lip into her teeth. Then just as quickly as he had appeared, he ripped his hand away from her mouth and darted toward the back pool gate. The one closest to the carriage house. It banged shut behind him.

Relief and dread twined up her spine as she gulped in fresh air. She unfolded the piece of paper in her hand. In the dim light she couldn't mistake the image. The smiling face belonged to her.

The photo from the newspaper article in today's paper.

She pushed to her feet on shaky legs—to find James—when a bloodcurdling scream rent the night air.

THREE

The smile on James's face felt frozen. Schmoozing potential investors wasn't in his nature, but if it was important to Medlink, it was important to him. His grandfather's company had a trickle-down effect on the economy in little Orchard Gardens—including the clinic—and he didn't have the luxury of allowing his discomfort to get in the way.

When the man he was talking to paused, James saw his opening and clapped the gentleman's shoulder. "Nice to see you again, Peter. I hope you're having a good time."

Peter held up his champagne glass. "Absolutely. Wouldn't miss your grandfather's party for the world."

James stepped away and a piercing scream sounded from the backyard. A flush of dread washed over him.

Lily.

Weaving through the crowd, he burst through

the open French doors onto the patio. His gaze darted around the empty space. He ran toward the pool and yanked open the gate, sending it crashing against the fence with a thunderous clatter.

Lily emerged from behind the thick evergreens. He clutched her arms, perhaps a little too possessively. A mild tremble rippled through her. "Are you okay?"

Lily looked at him with bright eyes. "I didn't scream." She lifted a shaky hand toward the carriage house. "It came from back there. Go check it out. I'll be fine."

James gave her a cynical look. "Go," she said, this time more adamant. "The scream came from near the carriage house."

"Go inside." He nudged her toward the patio. "I'll be right back."

She nodded and hobbled to the gate in one shoe. Confident she'd have company on the patio—guests had spilled outside at the sound of the scream—he jogged toward the back gate, wishing he was armed. He slowed, scanning his surroundings, not wanting to be taken by surprise. Serving in the army, he had grown to hate surprises.

On the pathway leading from the pool to the carriage house, he found Edna, the housekeeper, scrambling to her feet. He offered her a hand, helping her up.

"Oh, dear, I don't know where he came from." Edna brushed the back of her gray uniform with a few efficient strokes, seemingly equal parts afraid and annoyed.

"What happened?" He squinted into the dark yard, not daring to let his guard down.

"Someone raced out of the pool area and knocked me down." The light mounted on the outside of the carriage house caught the perturbed expression on her features. "He was in a mighty hurry. You'd think his hair was on fire."

"Are you hurt?"

"No, I'm fine." She gave the back of her uniform another swift swat. "Sometimes there's a perk to being pleasantly plump."

James laughed. Edna had always been a ray of sunshine. Tonight was no exception. He slipped his arm through the crook of her elbow and guided her through the pool area toward the house. He scooped up Lily's one shoe from the lounge chair as they passed and handed it to her when they reached the patio.

James pulled out a chair from a table, but Edna refused to sit. She glanced nervously toward the French doors. "Miss Elinor won't like all this commotion during the party." Many guests with drinks in hand had trickled outside to investigate as if the O'Reillys had thought to provide both dinner and a show. "I must get back to work. The cake needs to be cut."

"Please sit, Edna." Lily tapped the back of the chair.

The older woman gave Lily an uncertain smile.

Edna seemed to relax her shoulders. "Only for a minute. Until I catch my breath." Apparently satisfied that she would sit only for a moment, Edna settled into the chair. She ran her palms along the skirt of her uniform. "I don't know where he came from. I was bringing something to the carriage house." She searched past James, a wary expression in her eyes. "He startled me so." She hiked her chin, trying to muster a sense of decorum.

"Don't worry about them." Lily pulled up a chair and sat next to her, tucking her bare foot under the chair. "Are you hurt in any way?" Lily reached out and took Edna's hand.

"Oh, I'm fine." Edna stood up, dismissing all the attention.

The murmuring on the patio grew louder. The crowd parted and Elinor appeared in her exquisite purple gown with a pinched expression on her face. A few steps behind, Stephanie guided her grandfather by the elbow. His grandfather not so gently cleared the path with a thwack of his mahogany cane on the concrete.

No doubt Elinor's cool gaze soaked in every last detail, from Lily's missing shoe to her housekeeper, who seemed to be the center of attention. A look of disgust creased his grandmother's forehead. "What's going on?" She tipped her head back and squinted at Edna through her bifocals. With a neutral expression, his grandfather did the same.

"It seems we've had a trespasser on the property," James said. "He knocked Edna to the ground." His focus drifted to Lily, who sat ramrod straight. He was eager to talk to her alone. He knew in his gut something had happened before the intruder reached Edna.

"I ran to the carriage house real quick. I had to—" Edna wrung her clasped hands.

His grandmother held up her hand to silence her housekeeper. "No one's hurt?"

"No, Miss Elinor, I'm fine. I'll get to work on the cake." As if everything had been settled, Edna ducked her head and scurried around to the side of the house to the kitchen entrance.

"I'll call the police." James slipped his cell phone from the jacket of his dress uniform.

His grandfather lifted a shaky hand. "No. No police. It was probably just some kid cutting through the yards. Let's not ruin the evening. I don't want our guests hassled by the police."

Lily caught James's gaze, but didn't say anything. His grandparents didn't know about the incident at the clinic yet.

"Did anyone else see him?" Stephanie spoke for the first time. His cousin showed little to no emotion as she scanned the faces and stopped on Lily's. "Were all these people outside when Edna screamed?"

"I don't think so," Lily said. "I was by the pool. I saw him. I'm sure I could identify him to the police." She ran her fingers through the ends of her hair. "I was sitting by the hot tub when he…he came through the pool area."

The way she hesitated gave James pause. "Did he say something to you?"

"Yes, but…" Lily flicked her glance toward his grandparents. "Maybe we should talk in private."

His grandfather stomped his cane. "What is going on here?"

James gave her a subtle nod. Lily handed him the news clipping crumpled in her hand. As James glanced down at the photo of Lily, she said, "He told me he knew who I was." The night air suddenly seemed heavy, stifling. James struggled to catch a decent breath as a realization took shape. "He said he could get to me whenever he wanted." She rubbed her palms along her forearms and concern settled in her eyes. "It was him."

James pulled at his collar to loosen it. "The man who attacked you at the clinic?"

His grandmother gasped.

James reached out and wrapped his arm around his grandmother when what he really wanted was to pull Lily into an embrace, to reassure her he'd never let anything happen to her.

James gave his family the short version of what had happened behind the clinic this afternoon and made sure he finished by reassuring them. "Everything's fine. The clinic is secure. Every*one* is fine." James gave his grandmother's shoulder a little squeeze. "My old friend Chief Farley came to the clinic. The police will keep an eye on the place."

His grandmother touched Lily's arm. "Are you okay, dear? You must have been terrified."

"I'm fine, really." Lily's smile seemed forced.

"You never told us," his grandfather said, his voice both incensed and shaky.

"We didn't want to worry you." James met his grandfather's hardened gaze.

His grandmother's expression softened and her lips tilted into the smile reserved for her one true love. She patted her husband's hand. "It's okay, dear. I'm sure he would have told us soon."

She sighed. "Thank goodness you'll be coming to Medlink to work. I hear so many stories on the news of people trying to steal pharmaceuticals from clinics or drugstores. It's a scary world out there." She covered her lips with her fingertips, then pulled them away. "I'm so glad you're home, James. Where you're meant to be. At Medlink."

James choked back any words of disagreement. Now was not the time.

His grandmother frowned and flicked her wrist. The twinkling lights on the fence caught the diamond on her finger. "Enough of this drama already. You call your friend at the police station and let him know what happened here tonight." She waved her finger. "But we don't want any of our guests hassled."

"I'll alert Medlink's security. There won't be any more problems here," his grandfather said, as if saying so would make it true.

His grandfather tapped his cane on the stamped concrete. "Come on, Elinor. I have a birthday to celebrate." His wife took his arm and they rejoined their guests. From James's vantage point, he saw his grandparents chatting good-naturedly with their guests, no doubt reassuring them the incident was nothing more than a nuisance.

Stephanie planted her fist on her hip. "Thank

goodness you're both okay." She tipped her head to study Lily's face. "Why do you think he came after you here? It seems rather strange." A faraway look descended into her eyes. "I thought the incident at the clinic was random, gang-zrelated activity. Why risk coming here?"

Lily caught James's eye. He detected a wariness in her gaze. "To scare me into keeping my mouth shut. To stop me from identifying him." A question laced her tone.

James ran his knuckles across the back of her arm, reassuring her.

"I will identify him. He needs to be stopped before he hurts someone else." A whisper of a smile graced her lips. "I should have stayed safely tucked away in the lab. Nothing bad ever happens in the lab." Her quiet laugh held no humor.

Lily drove home to her cottage a few miles out in the country. James's headlights in her rearview mirror reminded her of the headlights tailing her on the drive to the party. She hadn't considered it anything more sinister than an annoyance, until now. Had someone been following her to O'Reilly Manor to threaten her? She rubbed a hand across her forehead, a headache pounding behind her eyes.

Lily relaxed her shoulders when she reached her driveway. She hadn't realized she'd been holding them stiffly until a pain shot down her spine. The gravel crunched under her tires as she made her way up the long driveway. Her bungalow-style home was set back among the trees. She'd loved this place the minute she'd seen it, her refuge away from the lab.

She parked her car alongside the house and climbed out. Keys in hand, she approached James's SUV, ready to thank him for escorting her home. When he pushed open his door and got out, she waved him off. "I'm fine."

"Please, Lily. I want to make sure everything's secure."

Lily tucked her chin in. "Since when did you become a safety expert?" Her rattled nerves made her snippy.

He waved a hand down his dress uniform. "U.S. Army Captain O'Reilly at your service." He took a step closer, hovering over her. She resisted the urge to reach up and place her palm on his chest—to keep him away or to bring him closer, she wasn't sure. "I was a physician in the army, but I was also a soldier. I know how to protect myself. And how to protect you."

She closed her eyes briefly, the memory of James training a gun on the thug at the clinic replaying on the backs of her eyelids. She drew in a deep breath. "I hate to admit it, but I'm still rattled."

"All the more reason for me to see you safely inside." Placing his hand on the small of her back, James led her to the front porch. Their footfalls sounded on the wooden steps, echoing in the stillness of the gorgeous summer night. Her feet ached with each step. He held out his hand for the key. She handed it to him and their fingers brushed in the exchange. James hesitated for a minute and her heart beat wildly as she wondered what he might say—what he might do. She bowed her head and studied the welcome mat.

"You should have left lights on." James's scolding popped the imaginary bubble of magic.

She squinted up at the dark overhang. "Oh… the bulb's burned out. I've never gotten around to changing it." She smoothed a hand down her cocktail dress. "Climbing ladders isn't exactly my thing."

"You live out here alone?"

"Yes, I live alone. Work doesn't give me time to meet anyone." She wasn't sure why she felt the need to explain. She didn't have many friends. And she wasn't interested in dating. Her work was her life.

"You need to be careful." The concern in

his voice settled on her shoulders like a cozy shawl. It had been a long time since someone had looked after her.

"Until tonight, I never felt threatened living in Orchard Gardens." She smiled at him, but couldn't read his heavily shadowed features. "Strangely enough, I do have a security system. The previous owners had it installed." She shrugged. "I never use it, though."

"You will tonight." James inserted the key into the door and seemed to have a problem with the lock. "Otherwise I don't want you staying here."

"You don't?" She snorted, in a show of bravado she didn't feel. "Last I checked, I made my own decisions." Before he had a chance to respond, she slipped in next to him. "Here, you have to hold the door handle and jiggle the key." She wrapped her hand around his and felt how solid it was. "It's a fussy lock."

He stepped aside a fraction. "Maybe I better let the master handle this."

Lily opened the door and reached in and flipped the foyer lights on, casting the family room off the entryway in a cozy glow, which immediately put her at ease. "Looks like everything's fine." Relaxing her body posture, she made her way inside and sat on the arm of the couch. A hot bath and her soft bed called her name.

"Mind if I walk around? Check things out?" James's intense gaze unnerved her. Did he think the guy would pursue her here?

Please, God, keep me safe. Let tonight be the end of things with that creepy thug.

"Be my guest." Lily flopped onto the oversize stuffed couch. Feigning nonchalance, she flipped through the pages of a celebrity magazine, although she couldn't name any of the so-called celebrities. Her sister must have left the magazine here. Cabinet and closet doors clicked and slammed open and shut. Lily tossed the magazine onto the table and slumped into the couch, closing her eyes.

A few minutes later a shadow crossed her face. James stood over her, an unreadable expression on his face. She shifted to the edge of the couch and faced him. "Everything okay?"

"Everything's secure."

Lily stood and adjusted the skirt of her dress. "Good. My address is unlisted, so I don't expect anyone will find me here."

She tried to ignore the cold chill running down her spine. "Well, thank you for escorting me home," she said, but James didn't budge. A hint of a shadow darkened his jaw. It would feel rough under her fingertips if she just reached out…

James crossed his arms over his solid chest.

His sudden movement snapped her out of her daydream, saving her from making a fool of herself.

"I don't like you out here alone. Couldn't your friend Kara come out and stay with you?"

"I'm sure she has her hands full helping Elinor wind down the party." Kara was an administrative assistant at Medlink and she doubled as James's grandmother's assistant. "Besides, I've been living here for five years without incident. I love this house." She forced a cheery smile. "I promise I'll set the alarm. I'll be fine." Maybe if she repeated it enough times, she'd convince herself.

James nodded, his gaze shifting to the large window overlooking the front of the house. She saw her thin reflection in the window and self-consciously smoothed a hand over her hair.

"Lock the door behind me."

"Of course." A small part of her was disappointed he didn't insist on staying longer.

"Night." James opened the door. Air from the humid night pushed in, mixing with the air-conditioning. "Make sure you lock this." He tapped the door with the palm of his hand for emphasis.

"Good night." Lily pushed the door closed and snapped the dead bolt into place. She rested her forehead against the cool wood of the door. "What are the chances I'll get any sleep tonight?" she muttered into the quiet room. She levered off the door and set the alarm for the first time. At least she remembered the simple code the previous owners had used.

She strolled to the large window overlooking the yard and watched James's taillights disappear down the street. Her front yard was cast in heavy shadows. She squinted, trying to make out the shapes.

A tree stump. A lilac bush. An overturned wheelbarrow.

An inexplicable chill made the fine hairs on the back of her neck stand on edge.

Was someone out there watching her framed perfectly in her front window?

She lunged toward the light switch and cast the room into darkness. There, now no one could see into her home.

She yanked the pull on the blind, letting it drop into place.

Would she ever feel safe again?

FOUR

Less than twenty-four hours later, James pulled up the long gravel driveway to Lily's cottage. He parked behind Lily's small sedan and stared at the bungalow-style cottage through the windshield. He could see it better now in the daylight. The empty porch dominated the front of the house. The landscaping was a little overgrown and the roof had lost a few shingles. If what Lily had said was true, she spent more time in the lab than at home. Not a lot of time to trim hedges and do minor home repairs. Lily's determination to find a treatment for the disease that had cut short her mother's life was admirable. However, it seemed unfortunate that it consumed her every waking hour.

He pushed the car door open and climbed out. He strode around to the back of his vehicle and popped the trunk. He scooped up the plastic grocery bags by their handles in one hand, then slammed the trunk closed with the other.

The sun hung low in the sky, but a good hour of daylight remained. He had hoped to get here earlier, but he had gotten caught at the clinic. Even on Sunday.

A huge cobweb hung in the corner of the porch, but no sign of a spider. He rang the doorbell and waited. Rustling sounded from inside and he shifted his feet. The white curtain covering the window on the door pulled back a fraction, followed by the jangling of the locks.

Good girl. Keep the locks on until this jerk is behind bars.

Lily opened the door, her expression wavering between curiosity and concern. "What are you doing here? Did something else happen at the clinic today?"

Her casual ponytail and makeup-free face made her appear even younger than she was.

He hoisted the bags. "Brought dinner."

Stepping back, she pushed the door open wider with her backside. "In that case, come on in." She reached for one of the bags and he batted her hand away. "How did you know I was home?"

"I checked with Security at the lab. They said you left an hour ago." He strolled through her house and put the bags on the kitchen island counter.

"Checking up on me?" Arching an eyebrow,

she tilted her head to mock-glare at him through her thick lashes. The sparkle in her eyes contradicted the feigned annoyance in her body posture.

"Can't believe you work on Sunday."

She shrugged. "I usually go to the lab for a few hours after church." She tipped her chin toward him. "What about you? You're working Sundays, too." She pulled down the side of the bag and peeked in.

"A lot of patients work during the week, so I like to have a few clinic hours on both Saturday and Sunday." He unpacked a head of lettuce. "I don't even have much time for church." It wasn't so much the time he lacked, but the desire. He had seen too much heartache in his lifetime to put much stock into church. An empty feeling expanded in his chest. His mother would be sad to know he had ignored the message she had traveled the world to spread. He shook away the thought.

He palmed the head of lettuce. "I need to make sure Medlink's star researcher is well fed."

"Ha. You assume I don't eat."

He slid a frozen pizza from the bag and smiled coyly. "I noticed last night you didn't have much in your fridge. Unless you count leftover takeout of questionable age."

She narrowed her gaze. "Why did you check

my fridge? Hoping to find an intruder in the vegetable crisper?" She slipped her fingers into the pockets of her shorts, crossed her bare feet at her ankles and leaned against the counter. "Really, now?"

"I opened your fridge because I was thirsty. I was looking for water."

She stretched across the counter and flicked on the faucet. Water flowed from the spigot. She held out her palm. "Ta-da…water."

He smiled sheepishly. "I'm still acclimating to being back in the good ol' U.S., where you can open the fridge for a midnight snack. After being deployed, it's a luxury, you know?"

"I can't imagine." She dragged her lower lip through her teeth, then seemed to snap out of it. "So you're going to cook me a frozen pizza."

"I figured you could use a home-cooked meal." In his world, heating up a frozen pizza counted. He opened a lower cabinet and found a large round tray.

Lily started giggling. Tears filled her eyes until they flowed down her cheeks. She swiped at them. "I'm sorry. I'm so tired, and the idea that you think a frozen pizza is a home-cooked meal struck me as funny."

Holding the scissors poised over the plastic seal on the pizza, he tilted his head in mock confusion. "You don't like pizza?" The scissors landed with a clatter on the counter. He started to stuff the pizza back into its cardboard box. "Then I guess I'll just take my pizza and go home."

She grabbed the box away from him, leaving him holding the pizza in its plastic wrap. "No, you're not getting off the hook that easily." She opened the recycling bin and discarded the box. She pulled out a chair from the table and sat sideways in it, resting her elbow on the back.

Something tweaked his heart at how comfortable she seemed around him. He pulled the plastic wrap from around the pizza. Small bits of cheese fell to the floor. She cleared her throat. "I went to the police station early this morning."

He paused. "I thought I was going to take you tomorrow?"

"I pushed your friend Chief Farley. I didn't want to wait." She crossed her arms loosely in front of her.

James put the pizza down on top of the stove and turned to give her his full attention. "Were you able to pick out the guy in a photo?"

She threaded her fingers through the ends of her hair and examined them briefly. "No. The guy doesn't seem to be in the system. They're going to call in a sketch artist. I'll have to go back when he or she comes in. Apparently, they hire a freelance artist out of Buffalo when the need arises."

"Sounds fair enough, but I would have gone with you." Part of him was disappointed she hadn't needed him to go with her.

Lily waved her hand. "I was fine. Besides, you didn't see anything. Well, except his mouth and chin under his baseball cap. I have to do this. I don't want this guy trying to get into another clinic or pharmacy."

"You did the right thing." He rinsed his fingers at the sink and stared out at the large yard surrounded by trees. She was isolated out here. He grabbed the cutting board poking out from behind the cookie jar and slowly chopped the cucumber for the salad. Her arm brushed against his. He glanced down into her bright eyes.

"Need help?"

"I like my space when I cook." He lifted his elbows and gently nudged her arm, earning him a fleeting, tired smile. "Sit. You've had a long couple days."

She did as he'd requested and crossed her legs at the ankles. A bandage still covered her knee. He sighed heavily, thinking about what could have happened yesterday if he hadn't heard the banging at the back of the clinic. He shifted his gaze to the window over the sink. The sun had dipped below the tree line, casting the yard in deep shadows.

His knife slid through the last piece of cucumber. Lily pointed at the cabinet over the fridge. “I keep a large bowl up there.”

“Thank you.” He found the bowl and scooped up the cucumbers, dumping them in. “When I’m finished here, I’ll replace the bulb on the front porch before it gets any later.”

“That would be great.” Lily grabbed plates from the cabinet and set the table. Just hanging out with Lily reminded him of all the things he had missed when he was deployed.

The simple things.

He had to enjoy them now. He planned to reenlist. Too many people needed medical help, especially the locals of the war-torn countries.

Pushing aside the thought, James opened the oven door to check on the pizza.

And he had no right to begin a relationship that was doomed from the start.

Lily picked up a piece of pepperoni pizza. She hadn’t realized how hungry she was until now. “Mmm, this is good, especially for frozen pizza.”

James looked up from his plate. “Go figure.” As good as he looked in his army dress uniform, he looked equally handsome in blue jeans and a collared golf shirt. Lowering her gaze, she stabbed a cucumber with her fork.

"I've always thought it strange how circumstances bring people together." She wiped her crumby fingers on the paper napkin.

He nodded. "I remember the first time we met."

Lily lifted her napkin to her face and covered her eyes, embarrassment heating her cheeks. "Don't remind me. Wasn't I scrubbing the toilet?"

James laughed, tiny lines forming under his brown eyes. "And I thought, boy, Grandmother is certainly hiring them younger and younger."

Lowering her napkin, she tried to suppress a laugh. "Sometimes on school holidays, I'd help my mom. I think I was fifteen then." She glanced toward the backyard and let the memory wash over her. "Before my mom got that job, I had no idea people lived like that. It was like a fantasy."

"My grandparents have done well for themselves. But my parents wanted something different for me." James plucked a piece of pepperoni off his pizza and popped it into his mouth.

"You never really talk much about your parents. Other than what they did for a living." For some reason, Lily suspected she was wading into shark-infested waters.

"What they did defined them. It defined me, too." He wiped his napkin across his mouth. "When we weren't traveling the globe doing missionary work and bringing health care to the underserved, we lived in the small apartment above the clinic. They didn't want me to grow up with a silver spoon in my mouth. My dad grew up in the mansion where my grandparents live now. He didn't want to follow in my grandfather's footsteps. He insisted on carving out his own path." He laughed, crumpling the napkin. "It drove my grandfather crazy."

He took a long drink of water. "As a teen I hated it. I thought people would think I was poor because I lived in—" he lifted his fingers to form air quotes "—the poor section of town."

"So, you moved into your grandparents' home in the rich section of town?" His background seemed a little hazy.

"Not exactly. My parents split their time between the clinic and traveling to underdeveloped countries to provide health care." He ran a hand across the back of his neck. "I wanted to be a kid. A normal kid. Go to school for a full year, you know? My parents finally agreed to let me live with my grandparents and go to the same public school I had gone to whenever we were in town." He closed his eyes briefly as he talked. One eyelid twitched as if he was fighting an emotion. “My grandparents wanted to enroll me in boarding school. But the deal was I got to stay behind and go to public school with my friends.”

“It doesn’t sound unreasonable.” Lily didn’t understand the obvious pain in his expression. “Teens want to hang with their friends.” She remembered how much she’d relied on her friends growing up, but they had all come from a similar background. Poor as dirt.

“They’d be proud of you.” She reached across the table and stopped short of touching his hand.

“I imagine.” He pushed away from the table and refilled his glass at the faucet. She wished she could read his mind. He returned to the table and sat.

This time, she let her fingers brush across the back of his hand. “You’ve followed in their footsteps.” She glanced at their connected hands, then pulled hers back into her lap. “Is there something you’re not telling me?” His mood had definitely turned somber.

He turned toward the back window. “Near the end of my sophomore year, I was in a fight at school. I broke the other kid’s nose. The school was going to expel me.” He pressed his lips together and paused, as if trying to find the words, or maybe trying to compose himself. “My parents had decided to give up their missionary work to come home and give me the stability that I obviously lacked." He sighed heavily. "The plane crashed." His voice cracked over the last words. Slowly, he turned to look into her eyes. The sadness in his made her heart break. "They were on the plane—the one that crashed—because of me."

Lily choked back a quiet gasp. The guilt James felt over his parents' deaths was palpable. She wrapped her arms around her middle. A cold, hard knot weighed heavy in the pit of her stomach. She understood his pain, his loss. His guilt, even.

He leaned back in the chair and studied the ceiling. "I've lived with this guilt for years. I owe it to my parents to make something of my life."

"You *have* made something of your life." She smoothed her thumb along the edge of the table, unable to reach out to him. His pain was too real for her. "You can't let guilt consume you."

"My head knows that." He pressed his fist to his chest. "But my heart..."

"What do *you* want to do with your life?"

"I enjoy working at the clinic here in town. Amazing how many people in this community can't afford health care."

Hope fluttered in her belly. What if he stayed in Orchard Gardens? Could she open her heart to him? Angling her jaw, she tempered her response. She had no right to consider a future with him.

Focus.

"But you feel a calling to reenlist?" she asked.

"Can I clone myself?" He laughed, meeting her gaze. "The clinic needs a new director. For now, it's being staffed by one full-time nurse practitioner. The rest of the staff rotates on a voluntary basis. The clinic needs some consistency in their staff. I keep thinking it will be easier to find a new director for the clinic than for the army to find physicians. The army needs me." He slapped his palm against the table, as if he had made a final decision.

"Maybe you should pray on it."

Something flickered in his gaze she couldn't quite identify. "I'm a little worried about Stephanie taking over as CEO of Medlink." He ignored her comment regarding prayer. Perhaps Lily had struck a nerve.

James continued, "Stephanie may not be as generous when it comes to supporting the clinic. The clinic wouldn't stay viable without Medlink's financial help. Stephanie's all about the bottom line. That's why I've held off telling her I don't plan to replace my grandfather as CEO until I can get some assurances from her—and my grandfather—that they'll continue funding the clinic."

Lily jerked her head back in disbelief. "Your grandparents have always been generous." They'd supported her all the way through medical school and she was only the daughter of their former housekeeper.

"Yeah, the economy is tough right now. Even on Medlink."

"I didn't know things were tough at Medlink. Your grandfather was the first person to offer me lab space to work on a cure for a rare disease very few people have ever heard of. They've always supported my research, even before they realized my work may have wider applications to treat other genetic diseases, too." Planting her elbow on the table, she rested her chin on the heel of her hand. "I still find it hard to believe they'd cut funding to the clinic. The work you do is so important."

"If your research has the far-reaching applications that you think it does, it will go a long way to securing Medlink's financial future."

Lily laughed and rolled her eyes. "No pressure there." She leaned back and crossed her arms. "I still can't believe my research for an orphan disease that only affects a small group has the potential to help scores of people with genetic-related diseases. It's amazing, really."

"And Medlink stands to gain financially."

Lily waved her hand. "That's fine by me.

My goal has always been the same. To help my niece. If your grandparents reap the benefits of supporting my research all these years, that's just icing on the cake."

He studied her face for a moment, the intense gesture unnerving her. "I suppose we've both been driven by our pasts." James pushed back from the table and stood. "Well, let me help you clean up and then I'll replace the lightbulb out front."

"Go replace the bulb. I'll clean up," she said, gathering the dishes into a pile while running his words through her mind. *Driven by our pasts.*

On Monday morning, James arrived at his grandparents' house bright and early. Charlie, their landscaper and all-around handyman, was watering the petunias. "Morning, Dr. James." Charlie had called him Dr. James since the day he'd graduated from medical school. He was like a proud papa of sorts.

"Morning. It's going to be a scorcher."

"You got that right, and you know how Mrs. O'Reilly is about her flowers." He hoisted the hose, sending a soft spray of water over the pink and purple petunias in the far back of the flower bed.

"The landscaping looks great."

"I could come by the clinic and put some flowers out front. Spruce up the place."

James smiled. "Not that the clinic couldn't use it, but you work too hard as it is."

Charlie frowned. "Someone tromped all over the pansies in the garden near the pool the other night. I bet it was the crazy person who gave my Edna a start."

"How's Edna doing?"

The gardener shook his head. "My wife hasn't been sleeping well. She keeps seeing shadows in the yard."

"I've talked to Security a few times over the weekend." James pointed to the side of the house. "The gate to the yard wasn't secure Saturday night. Anyone had access to the pool area. From now on, everyone has instructions to use the keypad for entry into the backyard through the gate. You also have a security system on the carriage house, right?"

"Yes. I've tried to remind Edna of that. She's a worrier, you know?" Charlie yanked on the hose, dragging it along the emerald-green grass. "The police chief any closer to catching this guy?"

James lowered his voice. "No, not yet. They're going to call in a sketch artist. Maybe Lily can remember enough details for them to track this guy down." The sooner this guy was off the street, the sooner James could stop worrying nonstop about Lily. Not that he'd stop thinking about her altogether. But he needed to know she wasn't going to be someone's target.

Charlie swiped the back of his hand over his sweaty brow. "What's this world coming to?"

"Just keep your eyes open, Charlie."

"Always."

James took a step toward the front porch and stomped the freshly cut grass from his polished shoes. "Don't work too hard."

"You know me, Dr. James. I don't like to be sitting idle." Charlie adjusted the spray on the nozzle, a concerned expression lining his sun-weathered features.

"Good thing you work for my grandparents, then." James smiled, then turned and pressed a few numbers on the security keypad next to the door. The light flickered red, then green. He pushed open the front door and the cool conditioned air came rushing out. A huge bouquet of roses, with a "Happy Birthday" marker poking out from a spray of green, sat on the foyer table, left over from the weekend festivities.

From deep in the house he heard Stephanie's voice. She must have parked around the side of the home and entered through the back door.

James strolled into the dining room and found his grandfather sitting at the head of the table.

"Look who's here." His grandfather's once

commanding voice sounded gravelly. He made no effort to stand, instead placing his hands on either side of his plate. He fidgeted with his silverware. He looked paler than normal this morning. Drawn. Tired. Perhaps the party and chaos had been too much for him.

"Morning." James shook his grandfather's hand. His grasp was not as firm as it once was. The concern for his grandfather's well-being niggled at the back of his brain, but he couldn't come out and inquire about his health. Although well intended, James's concern wouldn't be well received. His grandfather was a proud man.

"What would you like to eat, my boy?" His grandfather tipped his gray head toward the kitchen. "Edna will make you whatever you want."

A stack of pancakes and fresh strawberries sat in the middle of the table. "Pancakes look fantastic."

"Are you sure? She can cook up some bacon or sausage." His grandfather patted his belly. "Me, I need to cut back." His grandfather's plate was piled high with food, making James doubt his grandfather's *I'm-so-full* act.

"This is fine, really."

Across the table, Stephanie scoffed. "Grandfather, this breakfast must look like a feast. He's used to eating chow in the mess hall." She smiled brightly at James. "That's what they call it, right?"

James pushed his tongue against his cheek. "Don't knock what you've never tried." Actually, James ate better in the army than he did as a bachelor living in the apartment over the clinic.

"I don't need to try something to know I won't like it." Stephanie picked up the pitcher of freshly squeezed orange juice and filled the crystal goblet.

His grandfather cleared his throat. "I'm glad you're home. You did this family proud."

A lump of emotion formed in his throat. He had never heard his grandfather say as much. "Thank you." James pulled out a chair and sat to the right of his grandfather and across from his cousin.

"I believe—" his grandfather's authoritative voice cut through his thoughts "—it's time you came back to Medlink full-time. Stop running yourself ragged at the clinic."

"I suppose we have some business to discuss, then." James turned to Stephanie, her fork frozen midway to her mouth. It wasn't fair to anyone to prolong announcing his decision.

His grandfather nodded. "Yes, we do. Elinor has some crazy ideas about taking a cruise around the world and some other nonsense. It's time I cut back."

"I didn't think you had it in you," James joked, lining up his fork, knife and spoon with precision.

His grandfather raised a skeptical eyebrow, but didn't say anything. "We've been married a long time. She's always supported me. It's my turn to do something for her." The acknowledgment surprised James. His grandfather wiped the white linen napkin across his mouth. "It's time to transition the leadership of Medlink. Now. While I can make sure it's done right." His grandfather never used the word *retirement*. Instead, he referred to cutting back. Transitioning. Never retiring. "I'll be taking a position on the board of directors."

"A board of directors?" Turning her head slowly toward their grandfather, Stephanie set her glass down, her lips slightly parted.

"Yes. I have put together a board of directors to ease the transition. I realize it's not something done often with privately owned companies, but I think they will prove beneficial with their breadth of knowledge." His grandfather rubbed his fingers together as if he were trying to rid them of crumbs. "I will have a position on the board. The bylaws will allow the CEO to have a wide berth. But checks and balances are a good thing."

"And you expect James to be the new CEO?"

Stephanie asked, never taking her eyes from their grandfather. Expectancy weighed heavily in the air.

"Of course. That was always the plan." His grandfather met her gaze, unwavering.

"I'm ready to pull more of the departments under my leadership." Stephanie angled her chin. She draped her long blond hair over one shoulder and blinked her large blue eyes.

"I know you are, Stephanie, but I need to know James is on board." His grandfather shifted in his seat to square off with his grandson.

"You know where my priorities lie." James spread the white linen napkin over one knee.

"In a foreign country? Or in that clinic your father insisted on starting?" His grandfather ran a finger along his jaw and gave James that ultimatum look, the one he'd given when he'd been determined to send James away to boarding school. "It was okay when your father did it, because I was still in my prime. But you're needed here now."

"The people I serve need me." James kept his voice even. He cut a gaze toward Stephanie; her expression had softened. She seemed puzzled. His news must have come as a shock—a pleasant one, for sure.

"You should be proud of James, Grandfather. He's a great physician. Perhaps he's more suited to practicing medicine than running a business." Stephanie sat completely still. The air was wrought with tension.

"Thanks for the support, coz," James said, a knowing smile pulling on his lips. Then to his grandfather, he said, "I need to be up front with you. I plan to reenlist." Stephanie let out an audible gasp.

A steely gaze lit his grandfather's eyes. "There is a time and place for everything. You've already served our country. I didn't put you through medical school for you to enlist in the army." Little tremors shook his grandfather's head. The formidable man—a force to be reckoned with all of James's life—suddenly looked so very, very old. And it made James very, very sad.

Indecision forced the breath from James's lungs. "The army needs me."

"*I* need you. You must secure Medlink's future for the next generation."

James squared his shoulders. His grandfather never took no for an answer. Even now. He'd go to his grave yelling out commands.

"I don't mean to upset you." James softened his tone. "Stephanie is more than capable."

"Thank you. I believe I am." Stephanie set her fork across the plate and smiled.

His grandfather's gaze slid to Stephanie—his

red face registering his anger, the tremor in his head growing more pronounced—and back to James. "I think it's important Medlink has you at the helm, James."

"Grandfather, I went to med school to practice medicine. The only assurance I need from you and Stephanie—if I relinquish the position of CEO—is that Medlink continues to fund the clinic."

"Of course." Stephanie squared her shoulders. She reached across the table and covered Grandfather's hand. "We both know how important the clinic is, especially at a time when people can't afford health care."

All the dishes on the table bounced and rattled. His grandfather's fist sat rigid on the edge of the table. "You are the next generation. You're an O'Reilly. I expect you to return to Medlink as CEO."

"Wait a minute." Stephanie's voice grew hard. "I'm an O'Reilly."

His grandfather wiped his napkin across his mouth with a shaky hand and tossed it onto his plate. Holding on to the table, he forced himself to a standing position, the heavy chair scraping across the polished maple floor. He snatched his cane from the arm of his chair and leaned toward James, ignoring his granddaughter. "I have funded the clinic and I have allowed you to serve this country. However, the economy has been tough on Medlink. Changes are going to have to be made. Big changes. You're free to stay or go. But if you go, don't be surprised if you lose funding for your clinic. I'm especially concerned now after the incident there the other night. I don't want to be responsible if someone else gets attacked."

His grandfather took a few steps, his cane slamming against the hardwood floor. He swiveled and faced James. "And I don't want the incident at the clinic tied in with Medlink in any way. It would make potential investors nervous. What would they think if one of our star researchers was almost killed?"

James twisted his cloth napkin in his lap. A rock dropped in his gut. He had feared his grandfather would use that incident against him. He bit back any comments, knowing it would only fuel both his grandfather's rage and his determination to make a decision that proved he was still in charge. His grandfather had been generous. But he was also stubborn.

To get his way, his grandfather wouldn't hesitate to use threats.

James watched as his grandfather stepped out onto the patio and pulled out a wrought-iron chair. Edna, the housekeeper, must have anticipated this because she had his coffee and newspaper out to him before he had a chance to settle in. Stretching across the table, the housekeeper cranked up the dark blue umbrella to block the morning sun.

James released a sharp breath. "It must be hard for Grandfather to give up control after all these years."

Stephanie pushed her shoulders back. "Grandfather doesn't want to cut off the clinic. He's using it as a bargaining chip." Glancing toward the French doors, she leaned in conspiratorially. "He's not used to *not* getting his way. He wants to be able to control you. Don't worry. Go do what you need to do, whether it's the army or the clinic. I'll see that Medlink continues to fund the clinic. I promise."

"Of course you're going to promise me that *now.*" He watched his cousin. "You're getting exactly what you wanted. You'll be the head of Medlink."

Stephanie pushed her half-eaten plate of food aside and folded her hands on the edge of the table. "I've never made my ambitions a secret. Never. I've always wanted to run Medlink." She tipped her head. "Now we can both have what we want."

For some reason Stephanie's decisiveness unnerved him. "Give me a chance to talk to Grandfather again. Make him understand. I owe him that much."

Stephanie took a bite of a strawberry and chewed thoughtfully. "Fair enough. In the meantime, work on getting Lily someplace safe. We can't afford for anything to happen to her."

James let out a mirthless laugh. "How considerate of you."

"But it's true. Lily won't acknowledge it, but her life is in real jeopardy. Send her away on a nice vacation. Until this—" she lifted a shoulder as if searching for the right word "—unfortunate situation blows over."

"Do you really think I can convince her to walk away from her research, even for a short while?"

Stephanie's eyes darkened. "That's what I'm afraid of."

FIVE

Lily picked up the lab rat and cradled it in the palm of her hand, drawing it close to her face. The poor creature sniffed her hand, thinking it was in for an evening treat. She loved all animals—all of God's creatures—but as a scientist, she understood these rats were bred for research. To make sure pharmaceuticals were safe for humans.

"You know that, right?" she whispered to the rat, tracing a finger across the top of its head. She sighed heavily. A couple days back in the lab and she had been able to shake most of the stress from this past weekend's events. Even though it was already midweek, she was still waiting for a phone call from the police department to go in and work with the sketch artist. Once she did that, she'd try to put this whole situation behind her.

Tilting her head from side to side to ease the kinks, she placed her hand flat and the rat scurried onto the shredded paper on the cage floor. She latched the door and made a few notes. By nature, research was painstakingly slow. She prayed the clinical trials continued to go well. But her work in the lab was far from complete. Although a treatment was within reach, a cure was Lily's ultimate goal. Her beautiful niece's face came to mind. Thankfully, her niece had not shown any more symptoms in over a year.

God had truly blessed her.

She tossed her pen on the counter and glanced toward the door. Her lab was tucked into a far corner of the complex and not exactly the hub of activity. She hadn't run into James at all these past few days. Just as well. She didn't need any more heartache when he reenlisted. She rolled her eyes at herself. It wasn't as if he was knocking down her door to start a relationship. And when he did find that someone special, he deserved the whole package. A wife. *A mother to his children.*

Not her.

She shook off the thought. *Focus.*

Lily washed her hands and checked the clock. Her lab assistants, Sarah and Talia, had gone home hours ago. Or maybe they'd met up with some of the other young researchers at the coffee shop. Well, Sarah, the more social of the two, probably went. Talia had begged off more recently. Sarah speculated Talia had a new boyfriend. *Good for her.* Talia had reminded Lily of herself—all work and way too serious.

On Monday morning, her two assistants—who had been at the party—had been all questions about the incident by the pool at the O'Reillys, but by Monday afternoon, it was old news. Such was the digital age. Gossip about Lily's run-in had probably been replaced by the latest celebrity haircut. Or breakup. Or something equally unimportant. The short-term attention span of her generation was depressing, but no more than the memory of the creep's warning. Why would a gang member threaten her? Was it all just a ploy to keep Lily from identifying him?

Rubbing her temples, Lily figured it was time to call it a day before a full-fledged migraine took over. If that happened, she'd be useless tomorrow.

She left the lab and strode through the long corridor leading to the exit near the security guard. Long shadows crept into the corners of the mostly empty—but highly secure—complex. Glancing over her shoulder, she had the distinct feeling someone was watching her. She quickened her pace. A mixture of apprehension, nerves and exhaustion tightened her stomach.

She'd have to call Chief Farley and demand he get a sketch artist to Orchard Gardens by the end of the week, or she'd drive to Buffalo or Rochester herself—wherever the sketch artist worked. Until the thug who threatened her was in custody, she'd be looking over her shoulder forever.

The tiny hairs on the back of her neck prickled to life. Lily had never believed in a sixth sense until the day she couldn't shake the feeling that something was terribly wrong at home. She was in the middle of a final exam her senior year of high school and the overwhelming urge to leave and check on her mom drove her to distraction. Of course, she couldn't leave her exam. She was on track to be valedictorian.

Two hours later she'd found her mother dead in her bed.

The backs of Lily's eyes burned at the memory. *Stop it. You couldn't have known.*

The squeak, squeak, squeak of wheels rattling against the tiled floor caught her attention. Down a long corridor, the janitor was pushing a mop and bucket. She squinted, recognizing the young man. "Have a good night." The janitor nodded in response. Lily was careful not to step on the section of floor he had already washed.

"I think you're the last one here. Don't you have a social life, Dr. McAllister?" the janitor asked.

"I have a thing for lab rats."

He shuddered. “Their beady eyes give mc the heebie-jeebies.”

She flicked a wave. “Night, Brian.”

Lily strode toward the exit, swiped her badge through the security reader and waited for it to turn green. She gave a quick wave to the older gentleman manning the security station. He seemed preoccupied by something on the television. She pushed through one set of double doors, then another until she reached the outside.

Ah, fresh air.

The balmy evening air caressed her chilled skin. Bright light from the lampposts illuminated the parking lot. A jagged flash lit the night sky followed by a loud rumble, making her jump. A big fat drop of rain plopped onto her shoulder.

“Great,” she muttered.

Hugging her purse close to her, she bolted for the car, the only one in the back parking lot. She had parked along the edge of the lot under a tree. A drop of rain hit her head. Her arm. Her shoulder. The air smelled as if the skies were ready to open. She pointed the key fob at the car and nothing happened. “That’s strange.” She studied the key fob in her hand for a brief moment, wondering how she was going to unlock the door, before realizing she was being ridiculous. She had a key.

Of course—the key.

Feeling a little foolish, she inserted the key into the lock and yanked open the door. She slipped in behind the wheel and slouched in the seat, relieved as the raindrops danced on the hood of her car. Jamming the key into the ignition, she heard her cell phone going off in her purse.

"Hello?"

"Hey there." James's voice was like a soothing embrace. "Glad I caught you. Are you still in the lab?"

"No, I just got in my car."

He huffed, sounding frustrated. "Okay, I was hoping to catch you at the lab. Escort you home."

"I've made it home fine by myself the past two nights." Her pulse kicked up a notch. "I've been careful. I'm fine."

"Sorry," he said, his tone sounding contrite. "I got stuck with a patient at the clinic. Trying to keep up there and at Medlink has been tough."

"I can imagine." She watched big, wet drops splatter on the windshield.

A tension-filled pause stretched over the line. "Any chance we could meet to talk tonight?"

Lily massaged her temple with her free hand. "It's late." As much as she wanted to see him, she knew it was in her best interest to keep her distance.

"It's important. I tried reaching you earlier."

"I was in the lab." She felt as though they were talking in circles. When she was in the lab, she often turned off her cell phone to minimize outside distractions. She squinted against the streetlamp, her headache thumping dully behind her eyes.

"Please. It's important."

Blinking slowly, she realized James was hard to refuse. "Where do you want to meet?"

"I'd suggest the coffee shop, but I think they're closed now."

She squinted at the rain, now sluicing down her windshield. "Would you mind coming by my house?" She didn't want to go in and out in this rain.

"Not at all."

Lily turned the key in the ignition and nothing happened. Her heart sank. Her eyes darted outside to the empty parking lot. "Wait a minute." She touched the tip of her tongue to her upper lip. She turned the key again. Nothing. Not even a click-click signaling a dead battery. "Oh, great."

"What's wrong?"

"My car's dead." She gritted her teeth and wrapped her hand around the door handle.

"Are you in Medlink's back parking lot?"

"Yes."

"Hold on. I'm on my way. I'm not far."

"Thanks." She pressed End, then tossed her phone on the seat, annoyed with the delay. Leaning back against the headrest, she traced the automaker's insignia on the center of the steering wheel over and over again until she felt the imprint in the tips of her fingers. She wasn't used to sitting around doing nothing. She scooped up her phone, tapped a few apps, but quickly got bored. How did people waste so much time on these stupid things?

Out of the corner of her eye, she saw a shadow, a hint of something moving in the rainy night. Her head snapped up, wondering if James had gotten there already. Blinking, she tried to clear her eyes. She spun around, checking her surroundings. No sign of headlights from another car. Her hand slid over the armrest of her door and she flicked the lock control. Nothing happened. Panic sliced through her.

Right—no power.

She reached across and slammed down her lock and double-checked the other three locks, like a crazy woman in a horror movie. The steady beat of the rain plus the shaky sound of her breathing spooked her even more.

You're imagining things.

She wrapped her fingers around the cell phone, her connection to help. She could have Medlink security out here in five seconds.

With that thought, she slumped back in her seat and tried to relax. A second later, a loud crash sounded from behind her. She bolted upright and shifted in her seat. Her rear window was shattered. Instinctively, her hand went to the door handle. Her escape. She froze. No.

Someone was out there.

With trembling fingers she scrolled through her contact list, searching for Medlink security. Blinding headlights swept across her face. Tenting her hand over her eyes, she squinted. Her hammering heartbeat drowned out the sound of the driving rain. A blurry image moved outside her window. Someone was getting out of the vehicle. Lily stuffed her hand in her purse and found the leather case for her Mace. During her college days, she used to walk with it in her hand for safety on campus. She had thrown it in her bag after this weekend. Wrapping her fingers tightly around the cool leather, she realized now was not the time to wonder if it still had any efficacy.

The figure pounded on her door. She swallowed a yelp. James's face poked out from under the hood of a rain slicker. A relieved breath came out in a whoosh. She fumbled for the lock, then found the handle and pushed open the door.

"Do you have an umbrella?" he yelled over a rumble of thunder.

She stepped out of the car and into the soaking rain. "Did you see anyone out there? Someone just broke my back window." Her words tumbled out. She squinted toward the line of trees but couldn't see anything beyond the artificial light cast by the lamppost some fifty feet away.

"You're getting soaked." He nudged her by the elbow toward her open car door. "Get back in the car. Let me check it out."

"No." She shook her head for emphasis. "I'm coming with you." Rain dripped from her nose.

"You're staying here, where I know you're safe." A gust of wind pushed back his hood. He didn't seem to notice.

"Fine." Her fear had morphed into anger. She climbed back into the car, not bothering to shut the door. Getting wet was the least of her problems.

A few moments later James returned to the door with his cell phone pressed to his ear. "No, I think they're gone." He listened intently and nodded. "Okay." He ended the call and turned to her. The rain had slowed to a drizzle.

She sat sideways on the driver's seat with her legs propped on the frame of the door, scanning the empty parking lot.

"Are you okay?"

"Yes, but I'm about done with this nonsense." She reached behind her and unlocked the back door. She stood up and yanked it open. A brick lay on the backseat. She muttered under her breath. She scooped up the umbrella sitting on the floor of her car, shook off the broken glass and popped it open. She held it over both of their heads.

Huddled together under the protection of the umbrella, she jerked her head toward the back of the car. “How much do you want to bet that’s my friend?” Now she was mad, almost apoplectic. “Why does he keep coming after me?”

“I don’t like this at all.” A drop of water fell from his hair and landed on his nose. “He doesn’t want you to do the composite. Until he’s caught, you can’t take any more risks.”

The backs of Lily’s ears were on fire despite her soaking-wet hair. “Risks? I’d hardly call getting into my car after work a risk.” She said it with an air of confidence she didn’t feel. “I am going to meet with a sketch artist. Then they’ll catch this guy. Then life will go back to normal.”

“And until then…” He raised an eyebrow at her. The sky opened up again and the rain poured down on the umbrella, leaving the impression they were in a world all their own. She tried to ignore his close proximity.

She shook her head in anticipation of what he was about to suggest. “I can’t go into hiding. I have my work. Too many people are counting on me." She lowered her voice. "I am not going to hide. I'm not."

James gestured for her to get behind the wheel of her car. "Pop the hood."

Lily did as she was told. Wrapping her arms around her middle, a chill racked her thin body. She felt like a drowned rat. The initial surge of adrenaline had drained out of her. Through the droplets of rain on the windshield, she tracked James's blurred movements around her car. He checked a few things and then slammed the hood shut.

He jogged around to her side of the vehicle. Holding the umbrella over the space separating them, he said, "Come on. I'm driving you home."

Once they were both in his car, he scrubbed a hand across his short hair. Water glistened on his angular face. "Your battery's gone."

Lily plucked her wet shirt away from her skin. "Someone ripped out my car battery?"

"Yes." James ran his hand under his nose. "I'm going to call Security. Maybe they have something on surveillance cameras."

Lily glanced toward her vehicle and a chill penetrated deep into her bones. Suddenly, going someplace far, far away—where this thug couldn't stalk her—didn't seem so ridiculous.

SIX

Grateful to be out of the rain, James shook off his raincoat and hung it on the coatrack inside the mudroom of Lily's cottage.

"Brrr..." Lily kicked off her shoes and wrapped her arms around her midsection. She bounced on the balls of her feet. "I'm freezing. Excuse me a minute while I go dry off."

The familiar knot twisted his insides. He had spent his adult life helping people, but intentionally not growing close to any one person for fear of getting hurt. For fear of losing them. Like he had lost his parents. Like his grandparents had shipped him off to a boarding school after his parents' deaths.

Yet something about Lily was pulling him in.

He grabbed paper towels from the kitchen counter and dried the rain from his face. How was he going to tell Lily the news he had received from the police today?

"Go change. I'll make you something hot to

drink," he said, buying time. He toed off both his shoes and placed them next to Lily's.

Lily shivered. "There are tea bags in the little thingy on the counter."

"The little thingy, huh?"

"Yeah." She tiptoed across the hardwood floor, leaving wet prints, and pointed at a white ceramic thingy. She was right. "I bought it from my niece's school fundraiser." The hair around Lily's face had sprung free from her smooth ponytail. The dampness had created fine curls that framed the delicate features of her face.

He grabbed two mugs from the cabinet. "Now go. Get dry clothes on."

By the time he had two steaming mugs of tea on the small kitchen table, Lily had returned dressed in navy sweatpants and a university sweatshirt. Her damp hair flowed freely down around her shoulders. "The hot shower felt awesome." She slipped into the chair, wrapped her hands around the mug and breathed in deeply. "Thanks."

"Feel better?" He studied her closely. Her face was scrubbed free of makeup. She was beautiful. A longing constricted his chest.

"Much better. Thanks." Lifting the mug to her lips, she took a long sip.

"How much could you see when you were in the car tonight?"

"Not much. It was raining so hard. I saw a shadow." She set her mug down and locked her gaze on him. "It was the same guy, wasn't it?" A wary expression settled in her brown eyes. "Who am I kidding? It had to be. He's not going to stop until he's caught."

"That's what worries me." James ran a hand over his mouth. "The chief called me today. An officer in Buffalo recognized the symbol you described. The one drawn underneath the bill of the thug's baseball cap. It's a symbol of a known violent gang in Buffalo."

All the color drained from Lily's face. "Not what I wanted to hear." She pulled the tea bag out of the water and twisted the string tightly around her finger, then unwound it. She dropped the tea bag and a brown liquid slowly spread across the white napkin. Wrapping her hands around her mug, she slowly lifted her eyes to meet his. "I'm in real danger, aren't I?"

"I'm afraid so." He reached across the table and cupped her hand holding the mug. "I know you don't want to, but I think you should take a long vacation. Go someplace away from here. Someplace safe."

Lily's eyes flared wide, but she didn't say anything.

"Your life is at risk here." He brushed his thumb across the back of her smooth hand.

Lily slumped in her chair, letting her arms go limp at her side. "I've come so far with my research. I can't run away now. There's so much to do." She shook her head as if deep in thought. "I still have research to do. There're too many people counting on me." Her lips trembled. "My niece is counting on me."

He resisted the urge to reach out and shake some sense into her. "You need to think about your own safety. You'll be good to no one if you're—" He couldn't say the word. He hated to even think it.

She closed her eyes briefly. "I can't believe this is happening." Leaning forward, she rested her elbows on the table. She traced the top of her mug with her finger. "Have you talked to your grandfather or Stephanie? Medlink stands to gain financially from my research, too. What would they think about me going away?"

"I haven't mentioned it to my grandfather. I'm worried about his health." Couldn't she see her safety was more important than anything else? "Stephanie agrees you need to get away. Perhaps your sister and niece can go with you. I can't be responsible for something happening to you."

Lily pushed back from the table. "Since when am I your responsibility? I don't recall having to answer to you." Bright red splotches appeared on her porcelain skin.

"I care about your personal well-being. And if that's not enough for you, Medlink cares about your professional well-being." There, he'd said it. "Stephanie and I fear the implications for investors if something should happen to you." He'd do whatever it took to convince Lily to go someplace safe.

"Isn't that sweet?" Her tone sounded droll. She paced the small space, pulling the sleeves of her sweatshirt down over her hands.

"Take some time away until the police find this guy."

Lily stopped pacing and gave him a look of defiance. "I'm not going anywhere."

Standing by the sink in her kitchen, Lily turned her back to James and closed her eyes. Neither of them spoke. Nausea welled in the pit of her stomach. She drew in a deep breath through her nose, then released it slowly through her mouth. Pressing a hand to her chest, she opened the cabinet door and got out a glass. She filled it with water from the tap and took a long drink. Her nerves were shot. She had to pray for understanding. This was a cruel joke—to have the rug pulled out from under her. To have her world turned upside down. She stared out the window, not bothering to look at *him*.

"I'm really tired." She needed to be alone.

The legs of his chair scraping across the hardwood floor made her flinch. "This is only temporary. You'll be back in the lab soon. I promise." She sensed James approaching.

Tamping back the panic welling inside her, she spun around. "I'm afraid this might delay bringing Regen to market. I can't risk that. I *won't* risk that."

"I can't risk your safety."

Lily leaned back against the counter and wrapped her fingers around the edge of it. "What if someone told you that you had to close the clinic because it wasn't safe?"

James jerked back his head. She had hit him square between the eyes. That was exactly what he feared. His grandmother was particularly skittish after losing her only son in a plane crash. If she felt her grandson was in jeopardy, she'd pressure her husband to cut funding for the clinic. Fear made people react irrationally. Was that what she was doing? Was it irrational for her not to want to run and hide? Was it irrational for James to want her to?

James stepped closer and cupped her elbow. "I know you're scared. *Please* do this for me."

She grew lightheaded. She wasn't used to having someone take care of her. Ever since her mother's death, she had been the caretaker. The problem solver. Her strong faith had been her only constant companion, helping her achieve, to move forward, when a weaker person would have folded.

Lily bowed her head, resting her forehead on his broad shoulder. He reached around her and pulled her close, rubbing her back in a soothing gesture. She'd forgotten how good it felt to have someone to lean on. But that was all she was doing: getting moral support so she could plow forward. Nothing more. There could never be anything more.

A small chirping sounded from across the room. She slipped away from his embrace. Shaking her head in frustration, she grabbed her purse from the back of the chair and dug for her cell phone. She furrowed her brow at the caller ID. *Bethany.* Her sister. Alarm bells clamored in her head. Bethany never called this late.

"Hello?"

"I'm so glad you answered. I don't know what to do." Bethany's words came out in a breathless rush.

Lily pressed the phone firmly to her ear and strained to listen. "What's wrong? Is Emily okay?"

"She's been running a fever all day. I didn't think it was anything. I just kept alternating between fever reducers." The panicky sound in her sister's voice sent fear rushing in, pushing out any sense of well-being she might have felt moments ago in James's arms. "I gave her the last dose two hours ago and she's still burning up."

"Listen to me. You need to call her doctor and tell the answering service what's going on." The thought of little Emily in pain made her stomach hurt.

Bethany sobbed. "That's the problem. She doesn't have a doctor."

"What? Who's been monitoring her symptoms?"

"I couldn't afford health insurance after I lost my job."

"You told me you were covered until the end of this year. Then I was going to pick up the insurance for her." The pounding in Lily's head ratcheted up a notch.

"I misread the papers. I'm so stupid," her sister berated herself. "I was going to tell you, but then this…"

"Forget about that for now. You need to get her to the emergency room. I'll pay for it."

"Emily freaked out when I mentioned going to the hospital." Her words broke over a sob, then she whispered, "I think she remembers last time." Her niece had had an extended stay in the hospital when she'd first been diagnosed. Lily's heart sank. Her mind raced with her options.

Pushing past James, she stuffed her feet into

her tennis shoes. "I'll meet you in the emergency room. You *have* to take her." Lily heard a muffling across the line, then a loud wailing. She must have told Emily about the plans for the E.R. Her poor, sweet niece. Bending slightly, she rested her elbows on the dryer in the mudroom and covered her eyes. She held her hand under her nose. "Oh, sweetie."

"I can't do this anymore," Bethany said, the anguish in her voice palpable.

A firm hand settled on Lily's back. She glanced over her shoulder. James's eyes locked on hers. "What's going on?" he asked, his voice husky with concern.

Lily stood straight, covered the phone and explained the situation. He held out his hand and took the phone. "Bethany, it's James O'Reilly." Lily fought back tears as she watched James's handsome face as he listened intently to her desperate sister. Lily's chest expanded with gratitude. "Hang tight. Lily and I will be at your apartment in fifteen minutes."

Leaning against the door, Lily stared at James in disbelief as she pulled up the backs of her tennis shoes. "You don't need to go. I can go on my own."

Gently touching her arm, James guided her out the door. "I want to go with you. You shouldn't go alone." When she didn't answer, he added, "I have my medical bag in the trunk."

All the fight drained out of her, making her legs feel wobbly as they strode to the car. She didn't question why James carried a medical bag when so few doctors did anymore. She supposed it had to do with his work at the clinic. He closed her car door and jogged around to get in his side.

Lily focused intently on buckling her seat belt with a shaky hand, fearing her niece was having a relapse. Lily swiped away a tear, grateful for the cloak of darkness.

Lily found it strange these old, run-down apartments looked so different at night—cozy, even. Perhaps the glow of lights and the flicker of a television set in every window gave them a homey feel. Or maybe darkness made her forget the window frames needed paint and the roof was missing tiles.

James found a parking spot in the back lot, near a Dumpster. He shut the engine off and turned to face her, breaking the thick, heavy, tension-filled silence. "How long ago was your niece diagnosed?"

Lily sniffed. "Two years ago, when Emily was six years old. She had a serious setback a year ago, but mainly she's been symptom free since then." She pulled the door handle and the dome light popped on. The compassion in James's brown eyes made her breath hitch.

They walked around to the front of the apartment building without saying anything more. Voices floated out through the screens of the open apartment windows on the humid summer-evening air. The soft breeze ruffled the hair around her face. She had been in a flop sweat since receiving her sister's frantic phone call and she counted the seconds until she laid eyes on her niece, praying it would calm her down, reassure her. She wasn't ready to admit it, but she was grateful to have James with her. She didn't know how objective she could be when it came to her niece.

When they reached Bethany's door, she was waiting for them. "Thank goodness you're here. Emily finally fell asleep, but I'm so worried about her. A fever has never taken this long to break." Her sister paused a minute and her eyes opened wide in surprise. "James O'Reilly all grown up." She seemed to regard him for a minute. "I don't think I would have recognized you."

James took her hand. "It's been a long time." Bethany had come by the O'Reilly home only a few times, resenting that their mother had to clean other people's houses for a living.

"I hear you have my sister working at the clinic."

"Yeah, I really appreciate her help."

"And I really appreciate your both coming over." Bethany stepped back to let them pass. Her attention shifted to his medical bag. "Two physicians making a house call. God must be looking out for me for once." Bethany smiled at him, a bright smile that beamed with her gratitude. The same smile that had gotten her out of Orchard Gardens at age eighteen, leaving Lily alone at age twelve with their single mother.

Bethany led them through the small apartment to a back bedroom, walls painted pink. The furnishings and possessions were sparse, but everything was in its place. Emily's legs were tangled in the sheets and her dark hair was plastered to her face.

Something tugged at Lily's heart. She had spent countless hours working in the lab, looking for a cure for this precious girl, but she hadn't carved out a lot of time to actually spend with her. She reached out and ran the back of her hand across the child's moist cheek.

Was Lily shielding her heart from another loss?

Only recently had she made time to do clinic work. Her life was out of balance. Guilt pinged her insides even as she mentally fashioned her excuse: her top priority was to make sure Emily's future was bright. Make sure she lived a healthy, long life.

Lily leaned over and kissed her niece's forehead. A whiff of baby shampoo tickled her nose. Her niece's dark lashes rested against her pale skin in the purple glow of a three-foot-tall tulip night-light. "She's grown so much."

Bethany stared at her daughter. Her sister's eyes glistened in the dim light. "She's going into third grade. Can you believe it?"

Lily shook her head. It seemed like only yesterday when her sister moved back to Orchard Gardens with a toddler while her sweet-talking husband moved on to the next pretty girl.

"Do you think she's…?" Bethany didn't say what was on all of their minds.

"She'll have to go in for blood work." Lily touched her sister's crossed arms. "It's going to be okay."

A renewed sense of urgency weighed heavily on Lily's chest, making it difficult to draw in a deep breath. The first tingling of a full-blown panic attack bit at her fingertips as the pink walls with the princess border closed in on her. She hadn't a moment to spare. She had to push forward with her research. James set his medical bag on the dresser next to Emily's bed. *And he wants me to take a vacation for my own safety.*

James slipped in next to Lily and sat on the edge of the bed, placing a hand on Emily's forehead. The little girl moaned and muttered something in her sleep. He reached over and pulled an ear thermometer from the medical bag. "What's her temperature?"

Bethany's thin shoulders shot to her ears. "I never took it. My thermometer broke. I mean, it wasn't that long ago. I meant to replace it, but Emily has been fine for so long. It just slipped my mind. Or maybe..." Her voice grew so soft Lily had to strain to make out the words "...maybe I had deluded myself into thinking she was never going to have a relapse." Bethany sniffed and ran the back of her hand across her nose. "When I touched her forehead she was burning up."

"That's okay," James said, compassion evident in his voice. "Do you mind if I give her an exam?"

"Please."

Bethany and Lily stood quietly by as James pulled back the covers and gave little Emily a once-over. Emily moaned a few more times before settling in. This man had found his calling. He loved children. Her heart quickened as she watched James tuck a small bear next to Emily on her pillow. He smoothed her sweaty hair with his strong hand before standing.

"The fever seems to have broken. I think she'll rest comfortably now." He reached into his bag and gave Bethany a card. "Call the clinic. I want you to take her in for some blood work. There won't be any charge."

A line creased Bethany's forehead. "Is it absolutely necessary?"

Lily wrapped her arm around her sister's narrow shoulders and squeezed. "Everything will be okay. We have to have faith."

Bethany's eyes drifted to her sleeping child. "I just couldn't bear to find out she's sick again." She pressed a hand to her mouth. "I'll take her to the clinic tomorrow."

James took the card from Bethany and scribbled something on the back. "Here's my cellphone number if you need anything or if you have any concerns. Anything."

Her sister smiled, her wet cheeks glistening in the dull light. "You're not so bad for some rich kid."

James put the thermometer away and closed his medical bag. "So I hear."

Lily kissed her sister's cheek. "We'll let you get some rest."

"I can't thank you enough," Bethany said to James and Lily. "I really can't."

James stepped into the narrow hallway. "How are you going to get to the clinic?"

Bethany turned the business card over in her hand. "This is on a bus route, right?"

"Yes, but I'll pick you up so you don't have

to take Emily on a bus. It will be more comfortable for her."

Bethany pressed the back of her hand to her forehead as if trying to think of a reason to decline his offer. "Thank you. I hate relying on other people. But..." She hesitated a minute, obviously swallowing her pride for the benefit of her daughter. "Thank you. I am truly blessed."

After they squared away all the details, Lily followed James outside. "Thank you."

"Of course." James turned to face her under the yellow light of the lamppost.

"Now do you understand why I can't run away? My research is too important." Lily paused a minute. "Emily doesn't have time to spare."

James's eye twitched. "Regen will be on the market soon."

Lily shook her head. "A treatment is a wonderful start. But I'm still looking for a cure."

SEVEN

Lily seemed unusually quiet as James drove her home. He didn't bother to fill the silence. He dreaded the decision ahead of him. Undoubtedly, her emotions overrode her common sense because she refused to leave town. To go someplace safe until this lunatic was caught. It certainly didn't help that her niece's illness was a stark reminder of how desperately Lily wanted to find a cure.

It was more than work for her; it was personal.

He blinked against the headlights approaching on the darkened road. No matter what, he wouldn't allow her to be a sitting duck. He'd have to find a way to protect her, even against her will.

Deep down James wished he knew how to rely on God. To ask for guidance. But he didn't. Didn't know if it mattered anyway. His parents had been strong in their faith. They'd lived their faith. Yet they'd been snatched away in their prime in a plane crash. None of it made sense to him. Wasn't God supposed to protect them? His headlight beams swept across two deer on the side of the road, ready to cross. He tapped the brakes, startled out of his musing.

Lily gasped. "Deer out here make me nervous. I'm afraid of hitting one."

"You have to be careful." For far more sinister reasons than the wildlife. But he kept the last thought to himself.

"Well, I'm glad you're driving." She laughed quietly. "I can't thank you enough for checking on Emily. I appreciated having the extra set of eyes. I was too emotional to examine her objectively." Lily shifted in her seat. "I can't believe my sister allowed her health insurance to lapse. What was she thinking?"

James glanced over at Lily. She was staring out the window, her long brown hair flowing down her back. He shifted his attention to the road. "I'm sure she was overwhelmed when she lost her job." He softened his tone. "I see it all the time with my patients at the clinic."

Lily sniffed. "I sent her checks, but I should have taken the time to see her in person." She sniffed again. "I've been focused on only one thing—my research. I'm missing out on the day-to-day things. I'm missing out on Emily growing up."

"Don't beat yourself up. Emily knows you love her."

"What good is all my research if Emily's not receiving proper care?" Defeat edged her soft voice. "I've been working hard, but maybe I'm going about it all wrong. Maybe I've lost perspective." She slumped in her seat, covering her mouth with her hand. "Did you ever think you'd like to crawl into bed and stay there for twenty-four hours straight?"

James laughed. "I can hardly remember the last time I got six hours straight." Just sleeping in his own bed in the apartment above the clinic was a dream come true after years of deployment. He feared the longer he stayed in Orchard Gardens—the more comfortable he became—the less likely he'd be inclined to reenlist.

"Why do you suppose we do this to ourselves? Other people seem content to have normal nine-to-five jobs and a life outside of work." She sat up in her seat and tugged on the shoulder harness of her seat belt. "I spend all my time in the lab. You're splitting your time working both at Medlink and the clinic."

"Are you saying you don't have a life outside of work? You've never made time for a social life?" He flicked on his signal and turned into her driveway. He suspected he already knew the answer.

"Not really." The wistful tone of her voice made him pause. "I'm usually in the lab twenty-four-seven. You?"

"No personal life at the moment. Unless you call making late-night house calls a social outing." He glanced across the darkened vehicle at her. "Do you ever think you'd want more?"

He heard her quiet laugh. "No. I made that decision when my mother died. I knew I'd dedicate my life to research."

"But what happens when you actually find the cure?"

She hesitated a minute, as if she had never thought that far down the road. "I'll find another cause, I guess. What about you?"

"I feel sort of the same way you do. After my parents were killed, I felt like I had to continue their work, albeit in a slightly different venue. They practiced medicine as private citizens all over the world. I've done it through the army." He ran a hand across the back of his neck and looked up at her darkened house. He wasn't ready to say good-night. "Can I take you somewhere for coffee?"

"Do you want me to never fall asleep?" She laughed, this time with a little more humor. He liked the way it sounded.

"Don't say I never asked." He hid his disappointment behind a joke.

The cottage was set back on the lot, surrounded by trees. A soft light glowed from inside the window, but the porch was dark. Unease twisted his gut. Something felt off. He'd have to try to convince her to leave. If she continued to be stubborn, he'd have to settle for the alarm system and a night outside in his car to keep an eye on the house. Maybe guilt over his lack of comfort would finally make her relent. He put the vehicle into Park and turned the key in the ignition.

"Thanks again." She pulled on the door handle and the dome light popped on.

"Let me walk you to the door." He cast a quick glance at the dark porch. "Did you turn the front light off? It was on when we left."

"No." He heard the hesitancy in her voice. "Maybe there's a short and the bulb went out." She climbed out and poked her head back into the car. "I'll be fine. I'll wave to you once I get inside and turn on the alarm." She slammed the car door.

Despite her protest, James got out of the car and met her on the walkway leading to the front door. "I wouldn't be much of a gentleman if I didn't escort you to the door." Blinking, he adjusted his eyes to the darkness. Apprehension made the hairs on his arms stand up. Instincts from his years in the army kicked in. He scanned the property, looking for any sign of movement. The wind rustled the leaves on the trees surrounding the property. Nothing seemed out of place.

Except for the dark porch.

The moonlight reflected in her eyes with a hint of amusement. "No one ever accused Dr. James O'Reilly of not being a gentleman."

"Don't let them start now." He turned his attention back to the front of the cottage and the slightly overgrown landscaping. Recent events had him on edge.

As they walked to her front door, her shoulder bumped into his arm. "Sorry." He heard the smile in her voice.

Reaching down, he took her hand and squeezed it briefly before letting go. "I'll wait here and see that you get in." James hung back on the path and Lily paused near the porch. She fumbled in her purse for keys.

"Thanks again."

"You're welcome," he said, feeling more like a seventeen-year-old on a first date searching for something to say to prolong the evening rather than a thirty-five-year-old physician seeing a friend safely home. *A friend.* He put his hands in his pockets and rolled on the balls of his feet. A soft breeze rustled the leaves on the trees.

Keys jangling in hand, she climbed the wooden

steps, the old slats creaking under her weight. She froze and a quiet gasp cut through the night air. In two strides, he was next to her. Instinctively, he wrapped his arm around her waist and pulled her back. A dark spot, a lump, in the center of the porch came into focus.

"What is that?" she whispered, a quiet tremble in her voice.

He squinted into the darkness and the lump took shape. "It looks like a—" he leaned closer "—rat." James tightened his grip on her waist. "You okay?"

"Just great." Her tone dripped with sarcasm. She pulled away from him. Stepping over the rat, she jammed her key into the lock. Pushing open the door, she reached around the corner. The click, click, click of the light switch was met with more darkness. "Porch light is burned out again." Moving into the foyer, she flipped on the hall light. The interior light spilled outside, illuminating a ghastly scene: a poor rat, its head at an awkward, gruesome angle.

"This has gone too far." Lily's words came out clipped, angry. Her pale cheeks fired red.

His gaze traveled upward to the porch overhang. Someone had removed the porch lightbulb entirely. "Unbelievable." A muscle twitched in his jaw. He pulled out his phone and dialed the chief of police, his friend. Phone pressed to his ear, he strode to the edge of the porch, his shoes crunching on tiny white shards of glass. At least now he knew what had happened to the bulb. Leaning over the railing, he searched the side of the house toward the backyard. Pitch-dark.

He explained the situation to the chief and asked for more frequent patrols by Lily's house.

"Let's go inside." With a hand on her back, he led her past the grotesque remains of the rat and into her home. He shut the door and turned the bolt. "I'm going to check the house. Stay here."

A few minutes later he returned. Hugging her knees, Lily looked small sitting on the stairs in the foyer. "All the windows and doors are locked," he said, doing his best to reassure her. "You can't stay here all alone. I won't let you." He braced for an argument that didn't come.

Instead, Lily stared at him, an expression of defeat on her face. "What do you have in mind?"

"Maybe..." He ran a finger across his chin. "Let me check with Edna. Maybe you can stay in the carriage house behind my grandparents' home."

Lily seemed to consider it a moment. She grabbed the banister and pulled herself up. "I want to crawl into my own bed and go to sleep. I'm exhausted."

"I know. Go grab some things. I'll give Edna a quick call. After the chief gets here, I'll clean up the mess on the front porch and then I'm taking you to the carriage house for safekeeping. No arguments."

The next morning, the doorbell on the upstairs apartment of the carriage house sounded, and although Lily had been anticipating it, she nearly jumped out of her skin. She closed her eyes briefly and drew in a deep breath. Fixing a smile on her face, she pulled open the door.

"Sleep okay?" James greeted her with a smile, and butterflies fluttered in her belly. Inwardly she rolled her eyes. *Easy, girl.*

"All things considered." Lily kept her expression neutral. She hadn't spent a night in this apartment for years, not since after her mother had died and the O'Reillys had provided her housing between semesters at college. It felt comfortably familiar. She also felt safe upstairs from Edna and Charlie.

"Ready to take Emily and Bethany to the clinic?"

She grabbed her purse and they went down the stairs, past the beautifully landscaped pool area and through the locked gate to his vehicle parked in the circular driveway. Once they were in the car, Lily said, "I talked to my sister this morning. Emily seems to be herself, but I told my sister we should still bring her in. To run some blood tests."

"Smart move." James started the car, his smile warming her insides.

"Speaking of smart moves, do you think I was wrong to tell Chief Farley last night that I wanted to get the composite drawing done and then go public with it? We have to do something. I can't just sit here and wait." Lily hated the breathless quality of her voice, but now she worried plastering a composite sketch of this thug around town would only antagonize him. Last night it was a dead rat. Would she be next?

Lily fastened her seat belt and tried to relax into the seat.

A long silence stretched between them as James pulled out onto the main road. "Well, a sketch is one way of getting the word out. But—" he cut her a sideways glance "—you may become more of a target. If the chief's right, this jerk is part of a gang." His fingers flexed on the steering wheel. "My main focus for now is to keep you out of harm's way."

She squinted against the sunlight blinking through the heavy foliage. "I have to do it. I have to do something. I'm afraid of every little noise. I can't live like this." She rubbed the palms of her hands up and down her arms. "I want him caught. If his composite goes on the news—"

a new idea struck her "—maybe we can offer a reward. Maybe then someone will come forward and I can get on with my life." She ran a finger under her nose. "He's not going to stop. We have to offer a reward." She shifted in her seat to face him. "Do you think we can do that?" Hope buoyed her mood.

"I'll call the chief." James seemed resigned. "I'll push him to get an artist to the station later this afternoon. See if he'll contact the news in Buffalo and Rochester."

A tangle of nerves and excitement jumbled Lily's insides. Someone would come forward with a reward. She just knew it.

When they pulled into the parking lot at her sister's apartment complex, Emily sprang from the swing on the playground. In her matching lime-green shorts and T-shirt, Emily looked as if she was ready for a day of summer fun. She certainly didn't look like the little girl who had been sick only the night before. Her niece ran toward her mother, a little brown bear flopping behind her. Bethany took her daughter's hand and walked toward the car.

When Lily got out of the car, Emily let go of her mother's hand and bolted ahead. The heaviness of the past few days seemed to lift. Lily crouched down. Her niece wrapped her thin arms around her neck. "Hey there, kiddo."

"Hi, Aunt Lily. Where are we going?"

Lily looked at her sister, trying to read her expression. Bethany responded with a shrug and a little pout. Obviously, Emily didn't know she was going to get blood work done. Her sister probably hoped she and James would be a nice distraction.

Lily straightened and took Emily's hand. Her young niece watched James approach. Her little nose scrunched up. "Who's that?"

"That's Lily's friend James," Bethany said, smiling at Lily.

"Is he going with us?" Emily asked.

James crouched in front of her niece. "I'm a doctor and I came to see you last night."

Emily tipped her head, her bright eyes narrowed. "But I feel fine now." She moved closer to Lily, clutching her hand. Tucking the stuffed animal under her chin, she stuck out her lower lip. "Are we going to the hospital? I don't like the hospital."

Bethany looked like a deer caught in headlights. Her daughter's illness had taken a toll on her, too. "It's okay, sweetie," her mother said reassuringly.

"We're not going to the hospital," James said. "Would you like to see where I work? I'm a doctor and I have an office not far from here."

Emily nodded slowly, still not buying it. James

extended his hand, and her niece let go of Lily's hand and reached out for James's. Lily caught Bethany staring at her and lifted her palms in a *go-figure* gesture.

With a satisfied smile, James led her niece to the car. "You, your mom and Mr. Bear can sit back here."

Emily giggled and hugged her stuffed bear. "That's not his name."

James frowned. "Well, what's his name?"

"Just Bear."

"What kind of name is Just?" James opened the back door of his SUV and gave Emily an exaggerated smile.

"No, silly. His name is Bear."

"Okay, that works." He boosted Emily up into the vehicle. "Make sure Bear is buckled in."

Once they were all settled in the vehicle, Lily studied James, who didn't seem to be paying her much attention. He was so good with children. He'd make someone an awesome husband someday. He'd make an awesome dad.

Once they were on their way, he flicked a glance in her direction. His brow furrowed at catching her staring at him. "What?"

Heat crept up her neck and she quickly shook her head. "Just daydreaming." She shifted in her seat and studied the changing landscape. The country homes gave way to brick buildings constituting a small town that had seen better days. Several storefronts were empty. Glancing over her shoulder, she winked at Emily, who was holding her mother's hand. Lily really loved that kid.

Once they passed the center of town, they headed toward her childhood neighborhood. Her mother had rented half of a nondescript duplex. Not exactly located on the right side of the tracks. Some of the houses looked familiar; others had fallen into such disrepair as to be unrecognizable. One porch sloped forward under the weight of the junk stored on it. James slowed and turned on his directional. The first time she had come to the clinic, she was surprised to find it housed in a well-tended, green two-story home with only a small shingle with the words Orchard Gardens Clinic neatly painted on it. This was the only indication the home was actually a place of business. It seemed so cozy, quaint. Not at all the sterile clinic she had imagined.

Lily picked at a hangnail as James drove up the driveway and parked in the back parking lot. Her gaze was instinctively drawn to the pine trees bordering the property, separating the clinic lot from the apartment building behind it, shielding anyone who wanted to hide. *Stop it.*

Throwing back her shoulders, she opened the

car door for Emily. The child scooted out and took Lily's hand. Lily swung it playfully and smiled. "It's going to be all right, kid."

James led them around to the front door. Up a short ramp landed them in a standing-room-only waiting room. Nancy, the nurse practitioner, had opened the clinic only twenty minutes ago.

A baby wailed in his mother's arms. A few other kids played with beads on a curvy wire set up on a wood table. The adults nodded and smiled when James walked past. They all seemed to know who he was.

"Good morning," James said. "We'll have you back to see someone as soon as possible."

"Thank you, Doctor," the mother of the baby said.

Mrs. Benson, the older woman who had been there on Saturday, sat in a corner seat with her granddaughter on her lap. The woman looked absolutely exhausted. Lily noticed her first and went over to greet her. "Mrs. Benson, is everything okay?"

The older woman slowly closed and opened her eyes. "This one keeps me running," she said tiredly. "She hasn't slept well the past few nights. I'm worried the antibiotics aren't working."

Glancing over her shoulder, Lily watched James leading Bethany and Emily toward one of the examining rooms. She placed her hand on top of the older woman's work-worn hand. "Give me a minute and one of us will check her out. Sometimes these things just take time."

The little girl slipped off her grandmother's lap and reached up and tugged on Lily's hair. "Pretty."

Lily took the child's hand in hers. "Thank you, Chloe. Now sit here with your grandma. I'll be back in a few minutes." She cupped the little girl's cheek and smiled into her chocolate eyes. "Can you do that for me?"

Chloe scooted back into the empty chair next to her grandmother and ran her little hands up and down the metal arms of the chair. Lily handed her a Winnie-the-Pooh book. "I'll be right back. Do you want to read this while I'm gone?" The girl's eyes opened wide and her little chubby hands clutched the book. Smiling, Lily hurried down the hall and met the small group in the cramped examining room.

Bethany glanced at her. "I feel so bad taking up your time when you have all these other people in the waiting room."

"It's okay. There are two nurse practitioners on duty—" he glanced at his cell phone "—and a buddy of mine agreed to come in and see a few patients today. There are a number of doctors who rotate through this facility. Including me." He tipped his head toward Lily. "And your sister, of late."

Emily seemed calm holding her mother's hand.

"I'll step into the hall. Give everyone more elbow room." Leaning over, Lily planted a kiss on Emily's forehead. "Dr. James will take care of you, okay, sweetie? I'll be right outside."

"Okay." Emily nodded, squeezing her bear close to her chest.

Lily slid out of the room and made her way to the nurses' desk. The nameplate read Nancy King. Ah, the infamous Nancy. The nurse put down the phone and looked up at her expectantly. "Morning. It's Dr. McAllister, right?" The nurse smiled tightly, obviously too busy for idle chitchat.

"Yes, it is," Lily said, a little surprised because she had never met the woman. Lily had worked at the clinic only on Saturdays, Nancy's day off.

"Dr. O'Reilly told me you'd be in this morning."

Ah. "Can you make sure the bill for—" she pointed to the room down the hall "—my niece comes to me? I don't want the clinic to absorb the fee." Lily handed over her business card with her work address. "Please send the bill here."

The nurse studied the card as if she didn't know how to handle the request. The phone rang and the nurse gave her a curt nod before taking the call.

Lily made her way back down the hall as James was coming out of the room. A smile brightened his face. "Bethany is helping her get dressed. I drew some blood and did a quick exam. We'll have to wait and see."

Lily swallowed around a lump in her throat. "I've been praying it's not a relapse."

James touched her arm. "One day at a time."

Little feet padded across the floor. Mrs. Benson's granddaughter ran down the hallway and wrapped her arms around Lily's legs. Lily touched the tiny braids crisscrossing the little girl's head. "Hey there. Did you finish reading Winnie-the-Pooh?"

The little girl nodded emphatically. Something tugged at Lily's heart. Mrs. Benson, her arms full of her granddaughter's things, limped down the hall. "Oh, that child is going to wear me out."

James offered his hand and Chloe eagerly took it. "Come with me."

Mrs. Benson sighed in relief. "You're a lifesaver, Dr. James. A real lifesaver."

Lily patted the woman's arm as she passed. "You're in good hands."

The older woman smiled for the first time. "I know, dear."

EIGHT

Later that afternoon, Lily swiped her badge and pushed open the door to her lab. She snatched her lab coat from the hook and slipped her arms into the crisp, cool sleeves. Sarah, one of her assistants, looked up from the microscope. She tucked a long strand of silky, black hair behind her ear and slanted a sideways look in Lily's direction. "I thought it was some major holiday that I wasn't aware of."

"I had a family emergency." And the sketch artist at the police station had taken longer than she had expected. But the composite was done. *Done.* Maybe now they'd catch this creep.

"Everything okay?" Sarah sat on the stool and crossed her arms.

"My niece wasn't feeling well. She seems fine now, but James took a blood sample to be on the safe side."

Sarah seemed to stare right through her. Sometimes Lily forgot there were two other people committed to her research, as well. They may not have a personal stake in it, but they took pride in their work.

Sarah smiled convivially. "We're on track, Doc. We're going to have a treatment available soon. We won't stop until we find a cure." She tapped on the paperwork on the table next to her.

"From your lips to God's ears." Glancing around the lab, she realized for the first time that it was just the two of them. "Talia not in again today? That's unlike her." Talia had rarely had one sick day, never mind two in a row.

Sarah lifted her palm in a semishrug, distracted by something at her workstation.

"Did she call in today?" Lily's gaze darted to the phone on her desk. The red light blinked, indicating she had a message. She strode across the room and picked it up. She pressed in a few numbers, then listened to the messages. None from Talia or from Human Resources indicating Talia would be out sick. Lily buttoned her lab coat. "That's strange."

Foreboding, like cool air from an air-conditioning vent, skittered across the back of her neck. Sitting on the corner of her desk, Lily brushed her knuckles across her chapped lips. "Everything been okay with you? Anything strange happen lately?" A detailed image of the mutilated rat left on her doorstep scraped across her brain.

Sarah tapped the cap of her pen against her lips. “No…?” She took a step closer. “I mean, other than the excitement at the O’Reillys’ party last weekend.” A hint of fear flashed in her eyes. “I thought that was just some random intruder.” Apparently, most of the guests hadn’t learned of the intruder’s connection to the clinic.

Lily threaded her fingers through her hair. “It’s probably going to hit the news soon, so I’ll tell you.” She relayed the recent incidences. “The guy seems to be specifically targeting me, but all the same, be careful coming and going to work. My car was vandalized in the parking lot.”

Sarah’s ivory skin turned deathly white. “Just great.” She pulled her cell phone from her lab-coat pocket. “I’m texting my boyfriend. He can pick me up after work. I’m not going to take any chances.”

“I don’t think you’re in danger, but it couldn’t hurt.”

“Do you think this could be some radical animal-rights group?” Sarah tipped her head toward the rats. “Someone left a rat on your doorstep.” She paused to let that sink in. “Once we had problems at the university I was working at. Some psycho started harassing all the researchers.”

Lily focused on buttoning her lab coat. "I don't think that's the case here." She cleared her throat. "Unfortunately, I was in the wrong place at the wrong time at the clinic. I believe it has more to do with a druggie looking for a fix. Now he wants to make sure he doesn't get caught." And the jerk made sure she knew that he knew exactly who she was, making her feel vulnerable every minute of every day. Once again she cursed the stupid feature article in the newspaper profiling her research. Revealing her identity.

A new surge of fear swept over her. The news should be broadcasting the composite image soon. Had she done the right thing by pushing for the release of the image?

"This is crazy." Sarah shook her head, muttering something. She bent over the microscope, indicating she was done discussing this.

A nagging feeling haunted Lily. "I'm going to walk down to HR and see if Talia called in."

Her assistant's head snapped up. "Wait. Do you think Talia's in some kind of trouble?" Sarah fingered the top button on her lab coat. "I thought you said I'm not in any danger."

Placing her hand on Sarah's forearm, Lily said, "Let's not jump to conclusions. Maybe she called in sick." Fear radiated from Sarah's dark eyes. "Unless you know of anything else that might be going on."

Her assistant glanced down, then back up. She tapped a pen on the edge of the counter. "Talia's absence probably has nothing to do with her being sick."

"What are you talking about?"

"She told me not to tell you, but—" she hesitated a moment longer and tossed the pen onto the counter "—she didn't get into the Ph.D. program."

"Really?" Lily rubbed her forehead, confusion clouding her brain. "No wonder she seemed quieter than usual. She must have been devastated."

"You could say that." Sarah rolled her eyes. The two assistants had been known to butt heads. Sarah was well liked and had a quiet confidence. Talia was eager to please and boastful of her accomplishments. "Talia wanted to go to the state school so she could stay close by. Her mom's not in the best health."

"I'm surprised she didn't get in. She had good grades. I wrote her a strong letter of recommendation. I wonder what happened," Lily mused out loud. "Why didn't she tell me?"

"Talia was worried you'd fire her. And I think she might have been embarrassed. She told everyone she was a shoo-in for the program." Sarah picked up the pen and put on its cap. "You know what they say about counting your chickens before they're hatched and all."

"True, but she didn't have to worry. She doesn't need a Ph.D. to do the work she's doing." Lily's gaze drifted to the spot where Talia normally worked. Maybe Lily's letter of recommendation for Talia hadn't held as much weight with the admission counselors as she had thought.

Sarah folded her arms over her white lab coat. "She doesn't want to be an assistant forever. No one does."

In the middle of the day, the halls of Medlink's complex were bright and filled with people, a pleasant change from the gloomy atmosphere at night. Lily smiled and nodded at all the familiar faces, but kept her pace brisk. The employees didn't bat an eyelash as she breezed past. She was never known for her idle chitchat.

"Hey there."

Lily spun around to find Kara standing in the small kitchen nook in the front office. Her friend waved her over frantically. "Come here. I heard that guy who crashed the party has been relentlessly stalking you."

Lily pulled her arms against her body. *Stalked* seemed like such a strong word. But he *was* stalking her, wasn't he? She ran her fingers down the edge of her lab coat and forced a smile. "I'm fine, really. Thanks for asking."

If Kara had registered Lily's sarcasm, she

didn't acknowledge it. "Look over there." Kara jerked her thumb toward Stephanie's glass office. Muffled voices sounded through the closed door. "James and Stephanie are arguing."

James is here? She'd thought he'd be at the clinic.

"They're arguing? About what?" Curiosity made Lily's scalp tingle.

Kara lowered her voice. "I can hear a lot better when I'm sitting at my desk." She arched her brows. "But of course, Stephanie asked me for coffee right when it was getting to the good part."

"The good part?" Lily's pulse kicked up a notch.

"Stephanie wants you to get out of town. Like, yesterday. I'm only getting bits and pieces now because I don't want to make it obvious I'm listening. But she doesn't want you in the carriage house. She's worried you'll bring danger to their grandparents' doorstep."

"Seriously?" Lily's stomach hollowed out. "But my research."

Ignoring her, Kara tossed her long hair over her shoulder. "This guy actually left dead rats on your doorstep?" She turned up her nose. "How gross."

"It was one rat."

Kara twisted her lips. "Still creepy." She

glanced toward the closed office door. "Do you think the rat came from Medlink's labs?"

Lily slumped her shoulders and stuffed her hands into the pockets of her lab coat. Why hadn't she thought of that? Denial?

"Listen," Lily said, changing the subject, "did Talia call in sick today?"

Scooping the coffee grinds into the filter, Kara's face brightened. "No. You mean to tell me the queen bee of research is out sick? She must *really* be sick."

"Did Talia call in?"

"No. Maybe she's too sick." Kara went over to the sink and filled the coffee carafe. "Once I was so sick I could barely lift my head. But of course, Mrs. O'Reilly had urgent business I had to attend to." She grimaced and glanced toward Mrs. O'Reilly's office, which was next to her husband's. She didn't have an official job at Medlink. Mostly she ran social functions, but she still had an office. "Good thing I didn't toss my cookies on her expensive imported rugs."

"We're not talking about you, Kara." Lily gave her friend a close-lipped smile. "I'm worried about Talia. It's not like her to not show up for work." What if this stalker was targeting more than her? None of this made sense.

"Excuse me." Kara brushed past Lily and poured the water into the coffeemaker and set the carafe on the hot plate. "Maybe she had a mental breakdown from telling everyone how great she is."

Lily scratched the back of her head. "Talia's really not that bad, is she? She's a smart girl lacking just a tad in the social arena."

"You think?"

"Be nice." The smell of the rich coffee filled Lily's senses. "Do you know if Talia lives alone?" She found her gaze drifting toward Stephanie's office. From this angle, all she could see were James's hands and arms as he gestured to his cousin in what seemed to be a heated discussion.

"I think she might live with her mother." Kara opened the cabinet and pulled out two mugs. She glanced over her shoulder. "Can you imagine? And I hear her mother puts a lot of pressure on her. Talia's the first one to go to college." Kara shrugged. "Maybe that's why she always goes on and on about her research and her plans for a Ph.D." Lily detected a hint of compassion in her friend's tone.

Lily tore off the lid to a coffee creamer. "Am I the only one who didn't know Talia was rejected from the Ph.D. program?"

A flicker of a frown pulled at Kara's lips before she recovered. "You're always busy working. You rarely take lunch. The rest of us chat in the cafeteria. Besides—" she took the creamer and set it next to one of the mugs "—ah, I shouldn't say."

"What is it?"

"No."

"Please, tell me." Lily struggled to bite back her mounting frustration.

Kara leaned on the counter and braced her hands behind her. "Talia was upset because she assumed it was the letter of recommendation that was lacking."

Lily's chest grew heavy. "Why would she think that?"

"Apparently, she's supersmart, has really good grades—she certainly tells us all the time—so she assumed the letter of recommendation did her in. Maybe she's taking a few personal days because she's mad at you."

Lily smoothed a finger across her eyebrow. She had written a glowing letter of recommendation highlighting Talia's attention to detail. Perhaps she'd contact the university and see if there had been a mistake in the admissions process.

Lily turned to Kara. "Any chance you can get Talia's phone number? I'd like to check in on her."

"Sure." Kara lifted two mugs. "Let me wait for the coffee, then I'll look up her home number on the computer."

Lily hung back while Kara finished making

the coffee. Based on the posturing she observed in the glass office, the intensity of the discussion between Stephanie and James had escalated. After arriving at Kara's computer, Kara clicked a few keys, then wrote something down. "Here's the number." Kara handed the Post-it note to her friend. "Talia has also been talking about some guy. Maybe she's all tied up in a new romance."

"Missing work for personal reasons doesn't sound like Talia. Work has always been important to her."

Kara scrunched up her face. "You're right. Let me try her phone number." She dialed the number and waited. After a minute, she hung up. "Maybe she's sleeping."

Lily nodded. "Thanks. I'll try her again later."

The ache in the back of Lily's throat told her something was wrong. Very wrong.

James found his cousin, Stephanie, in her well-appointed office adjacent to their grandfather's windowed corner office. His grandfather spent less and less time here. James thought he'd never see the day. He ignored the nameplate to the right of his grandfather's. It bore the name James O'Reilly, but it had been intended for his father. Not him. Those plans had come crashing down when he was fifteen. Now—in his grandparents' eyes—it was James's turn to take over since his father wasn't around.

The thought of being stuck in a corporate office made him want to sign his reenlistment papers before he became trapped here.

Yet James also possessed a keen sense of obligation and a heavy dose of guilt. But just how much did he owe his grandfather? James stopped in Stephanie's doorway. She had on a tailored suit and her blond hair was pulled back in a smooth bun away from her perfectly made-up face. Seated in a rich leather chair behind an expansive mahogany desk, she looked comfortable. As though she belonged. A feeling he'd struggled to achieve for most of his life.

Stephanie slowly lifted her gaze from the paperwork in front of her. Her eyes widening behind rimless glasses, she flipped a file closed and rested her laced fingers on it. "What brings you here? I figured you'd be at the clinic." She turned her wrist, checking her expensive watch. James leaned on the credenza against the glass wall separating her office from the reception area. "We need to talk."

Angling her head, she pursed her red lips. "Something that couldn't be discussed over the phone? You've got me worried." Her gaze shifted toward the door, then back to him. She lowered her voice. "Security briefed me on the incident in the parking lot."

"Lily's had more trouble since then."

"Like what?" Stephanie's expression read intrigued, but not overly alarmed.

"Someone left a rat on her doorstep."

Stephanie slid her glasses down her nose and set them on the desk. "You have to make her go." She held up her finger and stepped from behind the desk. "Kara, would you mind putting on some fresh coffee?"

Kara pushed away from her computer. "Sure, coming right up."

James sat in one of the leather chairs. "Did Security get anything on tape from the incident in the parking lot?"

Stephanie closed the door. "No, the footage was blurry because of the rain. I told them to tie in with the police department to catch this guy." She leaned back on the edge of her desk and crossed her arms. "Lily's in real jeopardy. You *have* to convince her to go someplace safe."

James sighed heavily. "She won't listen to me. Her research is too important."

Stephanie stared off in the middle distance and shook her head. "You're friends with the chief of police. What does he make of all this?"

"The symbol Lily saw on her attacker's cap was a gang symbol. The most logical thought is that gangs were trying to break into the clinic for drugs. But why is this guy relentlessly pursuing Lily? If it's because he doesn't want her to identify him, it doesn't make sense. Every time he makes contact, he risks getting caught." He ran his palms across the arms of the chair. A growing uneasiness hollowed out his gut.

"Any chance the first attack at the clinic was someone targeting her—targeting Lily—and not out to get drugs?" Stephanie folded her hands primly in her lap. "Did that ever cross your mind?"

"No, it hadn't." He rose to his feet and crossed his arms, a muscle ticking in his jaw. "She's *lived* in the lab these past few years. She's spent all her time on Regen." He couldn't imagine Lily having any enemies. She didn't even mention having a former boyfriend. "No, I don't believe someone came to the clinic looking for her. Lily doesn't have enemies." He rubbed a hand across his jaw. "What about the gang symbol?"

Stephanie gave him a blank stare as if saying it wasn't her job to come up with every possible scenario.

"I moved her into the carriage house last night. I don't want her alone until they catch this guy."

"Why put her in the carriage house? You'll draw trouble right to our grandparents' doorstep."

"I've contacted Medlink security and the police. Grandmother and Grandfather will be safe."

So will Lily.

Stephanie lifted one silver ball on the pendulum set on her desk and released it. It smacked the adjacent ball, sending the one at the opposite end into the air. "Nothing's ever easy, is it?" She ran a finger under her bright red lips. "Why do you suppose this man is toying with her?"

James narrowed his gaze. "What do you mean?"

"If this man is really some big, bad gang member, why didn't he kill her when he had a chance?" She held up her hand to stop him from interrupting. "Sure, he didn't have a chance at the clinic because you stopped the attack. But why hasn't he taken the opportunity other times? At the pool the other night, in the parking lot… at her house?" Stephanie seemed to be deep in thought. "He had more than one chance to eliminate a witness. Why didn't he?"

James's blood ran cold, realization dawning. "He needs her alive."

Stephanie breathed out sharply through her nose. "I don't like this at all. You need to take Lily and get her away from here before he decides she's better off dead.

"If it gets out that our top researcher is being stalked… Well, we can't deal with the negative publicity. It's going to scare away potential investors." Her tone held both a hint of disgust and determination. "I've already taken phone calls from investors who witnessed the chaos at Grandfather's birthday party. I assured them it was nothing. Just a party crasher."

She gestured with her palms facing the floor. "Keep everyone calm." She levered off the desk and smoothed a hand over her skirt. "What are the financial ramifications if our rock-star researcher is killed?"

He gritted his teeth at Stephanie's matter-of-fact tone. She must have realized her blunder and added, "I'm looking at this objectively. Like a CEO. I want Dr. Lily McAllister to be protected as much as you do. You must get Lily to leave town."

He huffed his frustration. "She's not going to leave."

His cousin patted him on the arm. "I see she's out in the reception area. Go work your charm. Convince her to take a mini vacation until this madness blows over."

James opened the office door and forced a smile. "What brings you out of the lab?"

Lily tucked a strand of hair behind her ear. "I wanted to check on my lab assistant Talia York. She hasn't been into work for a couple days and she hasn't called in sick. It's unlike her." Lily lowered her voice. "And in light of recent events..."

"Did you call her house?" James asked.

"No answer." Kara handed Stephanie a steaming cup of coffee. "I made a cup for you." She glanced over her shoulder at James.

James waved Kara off and met Lily's gaze. Worry lingered in her eyes.

"Do you have her address? Let's go check on her." A coincidence like this sat like a spoiled bologna sandwich in his stomach.

NINE

The home Talia York, Lily's lab assistant, shared with her mother was a small ranch nestled on a street along a row of small ranches. They must have been built during a time when uniformity was in. All the lawns were well tended and flowers bloomed in the flower beds.

Except at the Yorks'.

The overgrown landscaping and the furniture stacked on the porch would have landed the ranch under the *TLC* section of the real-estate advertisements. Or on an episode of *Hoarders*. Renewed uneasiness swept over Lily.

"Are you sure we have the right address?" James pointed to the tall weeds hugging the side of the house. "This house has seen better days."

"Talia's too young to worry about landscaping. I understand she has a lot of student debt. Maybe they can't afford the upkeep." As if on cue, a lawn mower fired to life across the street. An older gentleman made a straight line across his lawn, glancing over at them from time to time.

Lily caught James's arm as they headed up the walkway. "If Talia's not home, we have to be careful what we say. We don't want to worry her mother." It wasn't unusual for young adults living at home to take off for a few days without informing their parents, although it did seem uncharacteristic of Talia.

James gave her a curt nod. She stepped onto the porch, testing her weight on the creaking planks. Through the open screen door, she noticed newspapers stacked inside the entryway. A television sounded from somewhere deep inside the house. Lily brushed a cobweb away from the doorbell and pushed the cracked button. "I don't think it works," she whispered.

"That darn thing hasn't worked since 1977." A shaky but firm voice floated out to them followed by a thud, clack, thud, clack. An elderly woman with a walker made her way to the front door, navigating the piles of junk.

"Hello, my name's Lily McAllister. I work with Talia. Is she home?"

"Well, Dr. McAllister, you, of all people, should know she's away on a business trip. Left a couple days ago, and in a mighty fine hurry, I might add."

Lily glanced at James, her confusion mirrored

on his face. She leaned toward the screen door. A whiff of something stale reached her nose. "I must have the schedules mixed up. Did she say where she was going?"

"Nope, never said too much. A friend of hers picked her up, though."

Lily tipped her head. "Do you know who?"

Mrs. York lifted a shaky finger to her eyes. "Can't see like I used to. Muscular degenerating or some such. It never sounded much like a good diagnosis, so I didn't pay no mind to its fancy name. Makes no difference to me what it's called. Doctors told me I'd be blind before my daughter gave me grandchildren." She huffed. "Might be dead before then because I don't think this boy she's bringing around is going to stick."

"I'm sorry."

Mrs. York waved her hand. "You didn't give it to me, did you?" A wet popping emerged from her lungs on her mirthless laugh.

Lily glanced at James, eager to get more information out of Mrs. York, but unsure of how to proceed.

"Mrs. York, I'm Dr. James O'Reilly—"

Mrs. York jabbed her finger in his direction. "You're the one supposed to be my Talia's new boss. I mean, boss's boss. Don't mean no disrespect, Dr. McAllister." The older woman plowed forward. "She told me about that fancy party at your grandfather's house. Must be nice." Her pursed lips accentuated the deep wrinkles around her mouth. "Also told me there was some excitement."

"Did your daughter mention when she'd be back?" James's smile had a way of disarming people, even if Mrs. York only heard it in his voice.

Mrs. York shook her head slowly, worry settling into her features. "Now you've got me wondering. Shouldn't you know when my daughter will be back?"

James shifted his feet. "Any chance she has a desk, maybe in her room? Maybe she made a note. We'd like to talk to her."

Clack, thud, clack, thud. Mrs. York moved toward the screen door. She leaned in close, her nose almost touching the dirty screen. There was a narrow slit in the corner of the screen just big enough to let mosquitoes in. "I suppose you are who you say you are." She flicked the lock on the screen door and pushed it open for them. "I don't see so well, so ignore the mess in here. Her bedroom is down that hall." Mrs. York stepped aside to let them pass. "I'll be sitting in the family room watching my programs. Let me know when you're done."

Lily resisted the natural tendency to crinkle her nose. The piles of newspapers continued down the long hallway. Trash littered almost every surface. Lily sent up a silent prayer for this woman. She was obviously overwhelmed.

"This is..." she whispered to James, struggling to find the words. She held her knuckles to her nose, inhaling her scented hand lotion. "How can they live like this?"

James shook his head but didn't say anything. The compassion in his eyes made her question her own. She shouldn't be so judgmental.

The door at the end of the hall was closed. A pink plaque with a kitten on it read TALIA in fancy script. Lily turned the handle, expecting to see a room as disheveled as the rest of the house. Instead, she found an immaculate room—sterile, almost. The bed was neatly made with a nondescript blue bedspread. Other than an alarm clock, there was absolutely nothing on the dresser surface. Lily let out the breath she'd been holding.

James brushed past her to Talia's desk. Not one piece of paper littered its entire surface. Lily hung back while he opened the desk drawers. She tugged at the collar of her shirt. The air in the small room was a little too warm and definitely stale. "Where do you think she went?"

He seemed to consider it for a moment. "Any chance she wanted to get away with the boyfriend, but didn't want to tell her mother?"

Lily scratched her head. "I guess. I don't know

her well enough. But why not use vacation time? She never struck me as irresponsible."

He pressed a finger to his lips. "We don't want to cause any trouble between Talia and her mother. Let's discuss this outside when we're done." His gaze drifted to the open bedroom door. The familiar notes of the *Eyewitness News* theme song drifted into the room.

James strode to the double doors of a closet occupying an entire wall. He slid them open. The clothes were hung according to color and were neatly pressed. Two pairs of shoes were lined up on the floor next to a cardboard box.

The extreme order in Talia's bedroom contrasted sharply with the disorder in the rest of the small ranch. Talia's apparent OCD tendencies would leap out even in a tidy home. Lily flattened her hand against her chest. "What do you make of this?"

"I don't know."

A scratching sounded from the box in the bottom of the closet. James glanced at Lily then crouched down. He flipped over one flap, then another. A large gray rat scrabbled up the side of the box, fighting for purchase on the smooth, corrugated walls. James glanced over his shoulder at Lily, one eyebrow arched.

"Did you find what you needed?"

Lily spun around, surprised the older woman's walker hadn't given them advance notice of her arrival.

Lily stammered before James scooped up the box. Rising to his feet, he slipped his hand around the crook of Lily's elbow. "Yes. Talia was supposed to drop off this box. Mind if I take it?" James guided Lily and Mrs. York from the room and pulled Talia's bedroom door shut.

Mrs. York stretched to see into the box, but James kept the flaps closed. "What do you have there?"

"Work property. You don't mind, do you?" James layered on his bedside charm.

"Oh—" Mrs. York's knuckles whitened on her walker, seemingly uncertain "—I suppose not."

"Did Talia mention going to visit any friends or family after her business trip?"

Mrs. York's face grew serious. "I'm all the family she's got. And Talia's always had her nose in a book." Her pale eyes darted around the narrow hall lined with magazines and plastic bags. She lowered her voice. "Not too long ago she brought a boy home. He didn't stay long. Didn't seem much her type, though." Her mouth quirked, and for the first time, her confident expression slipped a bit before she caught herself. "I suppose this wasn't much of a home to bring friends. I did the best I could. Her no-good dad wasn't good for nothing but drinking and smoking. Better off when he made himself scarce... better off." A faraway look drifted into her eyes.

"Mrs. York, do you have enough food in the house?" Lily asked.

The older woman's eyes narrowed to slits. "You saying I can't take care of myself?"

"Not at all. I imagine with Talia away, you aren't able to get to the store. Can we get you anything?"

Mrs. York's face smoothed. "I got plenty of canned goods to hold me over till my baby girl gets home." The older woman hiked her chin, revealing the loose, wrinkled skin of her neck. "She's going to take care of everything." The woman seemed to go someplace far away just then. "Do you know she wants to be a doctor? She'll be the first doctor in the family."

Lily swallowed hard, then forced a smile.

James pulled out a business card. "Please call me if you need anything."

Mrs. York waved her hand. "I'm fine. Just fine. We Yorks take care of our own."

Lily took out one of her business cards, too, and set it on the hall table.

James and Lily headed down the hallway. Lily froze in the family room. On the television was a sketch of the man who had attacked her at the clinic. A news camera was stationed in front of

Medlink. “Oh, no! I thought you told Chief Farley not to tie Medlink into this.”

A muscle ticked in his jaw. “I did, but the reporters must have done some digging.” He gently touched her arm. “Let’s go.”

Once inside the car, Lily ran her hands down the thighs of her khaki pants. “Is this negative publicity going to hurt Medlink?”

“There’s nothing we can do about that now. Maybe they’ll finally catch this guy and you’ll be able to put this all behind you.”

“I hope.” Her gaze drifted to the overgrown yard. “I had no idea Talia lived like this. She never told her mother she didn’t get into the Ph.D. program.”

“She could apply somewhere else. There’s more than one Ph.D. program in the U.S.”

“Yeah, but then she’d have to move away from her mother.” She shook her head. “I don’t think Talia would do that.” She glanced over her shoulder at the box in the backseat. “What do you make of the rat in the closet?” She reached between the seats and pulled back a box flap. The rat was still enthusiastically trying to make its escape.

James rested his elbow on the console between them. His arm brushed against hers. His clean scent stretched across the small space. “What are you thinking?”

A million thoughts. None of them made sense. "Sarah told me today Talia didn't get into the Ph.D. program. Since her grades are great, she alluded to the fact that maybe my recommendation was lacking. And maybe that was the reason she didn't get into the Ph.D. program." She jerked her thumb toward the backseat. "She had a rat in her closet. Maybe she left the dead rat for me because she's mad. Maybe it has nothing to do with the guy trying to get into the clinic."

James ran his palm across his jaw. "So obviously, Talia never read the letter of recommendation you wrote?"

Lily shook her head. "No, the letter had to be sealed. I dropped it in the mail room at work to be sent directly to the college, sealed. But I wrote her a glowing recommendation. I'm sure I still have a copy of it on my computer files." Lily slumped into the passenger seat.

"We need to give this information to Medlink security and Chief Farley. We can't let Talia back on Medlink property until we get answers." James turned the key in the ignition. Lily glanced at the house. The sheers in the front window fluttered closed as if someone had been standing there staring at them.

"Maybe Stephanie's right," Lily said to James when they reached O'Reilly Manor. "I shouldn't be in the carriage house. That thug's gunning for me. He'll track me down no matter where I am. I can't bring my problems to your grandparents' home…not again."

"You're not going home alone." James opened his car door and turned to face her. "And that's the last I want to hear about it. You're safer here." He doubted she'd agree to leave Orchard Gardens, and James was beginning to wonder if that would make a difference. This whole situation had him lying awake at night.

He tried another tactic. "My grandmother is very fond of you. She'll insist you stay, too."

"Thank you." A smile brightened her face despite the uncertainty in her eyes. He smiled in response, resisting the urge to reach out and run the backs of his fingers across her smooth cheek. It was good to see her smile.

She climbed out of her side of the car and met him around front. "Thanks for running by the lab. It's amazing we were able to avoid the news trucks." They had dropped the rat off. Lily had made sure it had a clean cage, food and water. At first glance, it seemed to have been shipped from the same source as the other rats used in the labs, but that didn't necessarily mean anything. There were only so many suppliers of lab rats in the Northeast. It could have been a coincidence.

An unlikely coincidence.

James held out his free hand to direct Lily to the front door. Stopping, she looked at the large double doors. "I can't stop thinking about something." She looked up at him with those eyes, those beautiful, worried eyes.

"What?" A soft breeze lifted the wisps of hair from her forehead.

"If Talia stole rats from the lab or did anything else she wasn't supposed to, all the work she's done for me is going to be suspect." Briefly, she closed her eyes. "It could jeopardize the future of Regen." She pressed a palm to her forehead. "All our work."

"I know." The thought had crossed his mind the minute he found the rat in the bottom of Talia's closet. "But let's not go there just yet."

Lily swatted at a mosquito flying around her head. Shoulders sagging, she seemed lost in thought. "I suppose you're right. One step at a time." She shook her head. "Besides, I can't imagine what that would mean for my niece if going to market with Regen is delayed." Neither acknowledged it, but the results of Emily's blood work were still out there, like a ticking time bomb.

"We'll get this straightened out." He entered the alarm code, then opened the large door. Strident clacking sounded across the marble entryway. His cousin, Stephanie, met them at the door, her long fingers wrapped around a television remote. "It's all over the news."

James and Lily locked gazes. He knew what was coming.

"Come here." Stephanie spun around without waiting for a response, demanding James and Lily follow her into the great room, where a large-screen TV was tuned into the news station. A well-coiffed newswoman appeared on the screen standing in front of the Medlink Pharmaceutical sign. His cousin pointed the remote at the screen and turned up the volume.

"...We have reached out to Dr. And Mrs. O'Reilly, but they have refused our request for an interview. According to witnesses at a gathering at their exclusive home on the escarpment of Orchard Gardens, an unknown intruder threatened one of their top researchers, Dr. Lily McAllister. This is the latest composite of the intruder." An image flashed on the screen. *"We will update you as more information becomes available. This is Candace Snow..."*

Stephanie pointed the remote at the screen again and it went blank. "Do neither of you understand the meaning of *discretion?*" She narrowed her gaze at James. "I thought you were going to handle this? Keep it under the radar so any potential investors don't get spooked."

James gritted his teeth. "Enough. We only

gave the police the go-ahead to release the composite photo and offer a reward. We emphasized the attack at the clinic. The news established the tie-in to Medlink." He smoothed his hair. "It was bound to come out sooner or later."

"Later would have been better." Stephanie flicked a glance toward Lily, then back at him. "I want to talk to you. In private."

Lily took a step back. "I know my way to the carriage house."

James whispered in her ear. "You don't have to go."

"I do." Lily blinked slowly. "I'm tired and you have to talk business."

Stephanie waited until Lily left through the French doors before whirling around on him. "We've got to do damage control."

"Damage control?"

Both Stephanie and James turned to find their grandfather standing at the bottom of the stairs.

Grandfather lifted a shaky finger, his skin an ashen gray. "What are you hiding from me?"

"Declan—" Grandmother descended the stairs behind her husband "—you are supposed to be resting."

Using his cane, he limped into the dining room and pulled out a chair at the head of the table.

"We didn't want to worry you." Stephanie

rushed over and patted her grandfather's shoulder. "We know you haven't been feeling well."

His grandfather jerked his shoulder and Stephanie's hand fell to her side. "I'm perfectly fine." He swung up his hand. The chandelier light caught the gold on his ring finger. "Don't patronize me."

James stepped forward. "The thug, the one that crashed your party and tried to get into the clinic, has continued to harass Lily. Today the news is broadcasting a sketch of his face. We need the public's help to get this loser off the street."

His grandmother wrapped her fingers around the back of another chair. Her large diamond ring hung loosely on her finger. She hiked up her chin. "That settles it."

James pulled his head back. "Settles what?"

"You're going to return full-time to Medlink. Now. No more clinic. It's too dangerous. These people are never going to stop." His grandmother pulled out the chair and folded herself into it. She placed her hands in her lap as if the matter had been settled simply because she had decreed it.

After a moment, his grandmother looked up. "You've done a lot of good. You remind me so much of your father." She slipped a tissue out of her sleeve and dabbed at the corners of her eyes. "I can't lose you, too. Please. It's time to leave the clinic."

James sat in the chair next to his grandmother's and took her hands into his. "Please, don't worry. It's no way to live." Perhaps her denial had made her forget his plans to reenlist. Tonight didn't seem like the best opportunity to remind his grandparents of his plans. In good conscience, he couldn't leave until things had settled down here.

He thought of Lily. He couldn't leave her. Not now. He'd have to have faith. *Faith.*

His grandfather made a sniffing sound at the end of the table. When James met his eyes, his grandfather stiffened his back. He carefully schooled his expression. "When is Edna going to serve dinner?"

"She has some groceries for Lily, who's staying in the carriage house," Stephanie said, standing over them with the remote in her hand.

"I'm glad Lily's here," his grandmother said. "It will be nice to have her around. I'm just sorry it's under these circumstances." Her gaze drifted to James. "It seems like you two are still spending a lot of time together. Are my hopes you'll settle down realistic?"

James laughed, glad Lily wasn't in the room. "We're just friends."

"Just friends?" His grandmother seemed to

consider this a moment. "I'm not buying it. Maybe after all this blows over you'll see what I can see. You two are meant to be together." She tapped the back of the chair. "How perfect. You can run Medlink and Lily can do her research."

Stephanie's features grew pinched. "Grandmother, James doesn't want to run Medlink. He wants to reenlist."

Their grandmother waved her hand, dismissing her. "I'm going to check on Edna. We need to eat. Your grandfather is tired."

After their grandmother walked away, Stephanie leaned in close so only James could hear. "You need to grow a backbone. If you plan to reenlist, do it, so the rest of us can get on with our lives."

Stephanie turned toward her grandfather and projected her voice. "I need to go back to the office and do some damage control after all this news coverage."

Grandfather lifted his hand in dismissal, much as their grandmother had.

Stephanie tossed her hair over her shoulder and strode out of the room. Her frustration rolled off her in waves. The alarm chimed a half second before the front door slammed.

Grandfather coughed in his napkin. "You need to return to Medlink. Stephanie does not have the temperament to head the company."

James opened his mouth to protest, then decided better of it. Grandfather appeared more frail than James had ever seen him. Stephanie may have considered her cousin to be weak.

He considered himself to be compassionate.

TEN

Right after a somewhat formal dinner with the O'Reilly family, Lily excused herself and retreated to the carriage house. A tense undercurrent had flowed throughout the evening that was at odds with the polite exchange of pleasantries. Apparently, no one was willing to share what was really on their minds.

Working off some of her stress, Lily cut the tube of cookie dough and placed heaping mounds on the sheet and slipped it into the oven. She could almost taste the chocolate-chip cookies.

Lily double-checked the lock on the door and plopped on the couch, picking up the remote. Maybe she could find some light romantic comedy to take her mind off everything. Relaxing in this quaint home had reminded her of the early days when she had moved into the carriage house right after her mother had died. Sweet Edna had made the horrible transition a little bit easier for her. In a way, it seemed odd Edna had been the one to offer comfort since she had replaced Lily's mother as the O'Reillys' housekeeper. The O'Reillys had provided Lily lodging and an education, but Edna provided the mothering she needed after her mother had died.

Lily dropped the remote at the sound of a quiet rap on the door. Anticipation bubbled in her stomach. She pointed the remote at the TV and turned down the volume. She unfolded her legs from under her and stood. She shook out the tingling sensation in her feet from the lack of circulation. Crossing the room, she snapped on an end-table lamp as she passed, chasing away the gloomy shadows. Another quiet knock sounded at the door.

She peered through the peephole and saw James's profile. A strange mix of relief and nervousness swept over her. James's intense gaze was directed toward the darkened yard. She unlocked the door and yanked it open. A slow smile spread across his face, warming her heart.

"Hey there." His voice was gravelly, as if the exhaustion from the day had caught up to him, too.

"Hey yourself." She hugged the edge of the door, resisting the urge to reach out and touch the dark shadow on his jaw. She was growing partial to this look on him. It made him appear rugged, even more handsome, if possible. She stepped out of the doorway and waved her hand in a sweeping gesture. "Come on in. I'm about to start a movie."

Amusement softened his features. "An action adventure?"

"Seriously?" She dipped her chin and raised an eyebrow. "I think I've had enough action adventure in my real life lately. I hardly want to be entertained by it."

James turned around and locked the door. Something about the deliberate gesture made her uneasy. "Do you think I'm safe here? Honestly?"

"Yes." He pinned her with a steady gaze. "I talked to Medlink's security, too. You're safe."

"Okay." Lily turned on her bare feet and hustled to the kitchen area, suddenly remembering the cookies in the oven. She opened the oven door. "Phew. Just in time." The sweet smell of chocolate-chip cookies floated to her nose.

She grabbed a pot holder and removed the cookie tray, setting it on top of the stove. She dropped it with a clatter and bit back a curse. The cookies bounced on the tray. Clutching her hand, she shook her head. "Yowza. Remind me to buy a thicker pot holder."

"Here, let me see." James held out his hand.

Hesitantly, she offered her hand. "Okay, Doctor," she said playfully. She leaned over to inspect her fingers, their faces inches apart. "It's only a little red. I think I'll live." An unexpected flush of warmth shot up her hand from where he touched her fingers. He gently ran his thumb over the pad of hers, which was a little redder than the rest of her fingers. "Do you have aloe?"

She pulled her hand away. "It's fine." She tore a piece of paper towel from the roll, then grabbed a cube of ice from the freezer and held it against her thumb. She glanced over her shoulder at James leaning against the counter, his shirt collar and tie loosened. She turned back around and closed the oven door. The expression *if you can't stand the heat, get out of the kitchen* drifted to mind.

James tipped his head toward the cookies, amusement lighting his eyes. "Taking up a hobby? I didn't know you baked." Using the spatula, he slipped a cookie from the tray. He broke a corner off and popped it into his mouth. "Good. And hot." He waved his hand in front of his mouth.

"I'd hardly call myself a baker. Edna remembered I liked chocolate-chip cookies. So if you count cutting up a roll of prepackaged dough as baking, I'm a baker." She smiled, then suddenly grew somber. "Things were pretty tense at dinner. Were your grandparents mad about the news coverage? I'm surprised they didn't say anything."

"They said their fill before dinner." He put the other half of the cookie back on the sheet. He sat on the stool at the island, leaning his elbows on the counter. "Nothing more than you already know. My grandmother's pressuring me to return to Medlink full-time." His cheeks puffed up and he released a long breath. "Now she's more adamant than ever that I stop working at the clinic. She's worried about my safety." His tone dripped with irony.

"They know I want to reenlist." He leaned his cheek on his fisted hand. "But I don't think now is the best time to push my plans. My grandmother's afraid for my safety at a clinic in Orchard Gardens. How do you suppose she'll feel about me returning to a war-torn country? I don't want either of them to make a rash decision to cut funding to the clinic to strong-arm me into returning to Medlink." He shook his head in disbelief. "I was hoping I could convince them Medlink is in good hands with Stephanie."

"You're not sure it is?"

"I…don't know. And my grandfather doesn't think it is." He picked up a pen from the counter, turned it over in his fingers and then tossed it aside. "I need to sit down and go over Medlink's financials. See the big picture. Since I've been back, I feel like all I've done is put out fires."

Lily placed a few cookies on a plate and carried them to the couch. James sat in a nearby armchair. Rubbing his hands along the smooth fabric of the chair's arms, he looked up at her with a strange expression on his face. "This is the first time I've been in this apartment."

"You had no reason to be, I guess." Lily took a bite of her cookie over the plate, careful not to get crumbs on the couch.

He studied her face. "How come we never hung out when we were teenagers?"

She coughed, nearly choking on the cookie. "That would have gone over great. James O'Reilly dating the daughter of the housekeeper." Her laugh sounded awkward in her ears.

"I never thought of you as somehow less than." Something akin to hurt flickered in his eyes.

"I suppose you were different. That's because your parents kept you humble. However, it's tough not to feel inferior when you're surrounded by extreme wealth." She put the plate down and tucked her hands under her thighs. "I helped my mother clean this house. I cleaned the toilets. It's hard not to feel *less than*."

"I never really thought about it."

"You didn't have to. You rebelled, but you had choices. My mother worked hard to make sure my sister and I had a future. And I'm truly grateful to my mother. And I feel God has blessed me by bringing your grandparents into my life. I would never have been able to go to medical school without their generosity. I owe them a lot."

A crooked grin transformed his face. "My grandmother is very fond of you." James ran a hand across his jaw. "She's ready for the next generation of O'Reillys."

"Ah, leave it to Elinor. Glad to know she's still looking out for me." Lily forced a smile despite the heat burning her cheeks. "I am indebted to your grandparents, but a grandchild wasn't exactly what I had in mind." She flattened her palm against the hollow of her neck and stood. "I need to get some water. Can I get you anything?"

"I'm fine, thanks."

Lily grabbed a bottle of water from the fridge and found herself drawn to the sliding glass doors. She needed air. She slid the door open and stepped onto the narrow balcony. She put her water on the little table and wrapped her hands around the solid wrought-iron railing, drawing air into her lungs.

"Is it something I said?" James joined her.

She tucked a strand of hair behind her ear. "I've been working so hard all these years. College. Med school. My research. Then one day, I'm almost where I need to be and some crazy person decides to harass me, forcing me to stop in my tracks and lift my head for once. To see there's life beyond the lab. Good and bad." She held up her palms. "Here I am. Thirty-three and…"

"Don't be so hard on yourself." His soothing voice washed over her. He pressed his palms to hers and intertwined their fingers. She froze and looked up at him. "You've accomplished more than most people your age."

Her gaze dropped to his fingers laced in hers. "My life is lopsided. Am I really living?" A little voice inside her head kept yelling, *Shut up, shut up, shut up.*

He pulled their intertwined hands to his solid chest. "I know how you feel. My parents' deaths… I feel like I've been living my life for them. I've wanted to make them proud. Sometimes I can't separate what I want from what I think they'd want."

Lily squeezed his hand, sympathizing with him. She sensed he had just shared something he had never shared with anyone before. "Oh, they would be proud. You've followed in their footsteps." She tried to read his expression. "What is it *you* want to do?"

Bowing his head, he lifted her fingers to his

lips. "Guilt is not a good motivator. I live with it every day." His breath whispered across her knuckles, sending her thoughts into a hazy fog.

She slid her hands free from his and immediately missed their solid warmth. "You have to learn to move past that. You can't blame yourself for your parents' deaths."

James shuffled his feet and braced his hands on the railing. "It's hard not to when I was the reason they were on the plane." He shook his head. "They were willing to give up their missionary work to come home and give me what my grandmother called a more stable home. I was such a punk."

"Don't do that to yourself. You were a kid. Do you know how many kids give their parents grief?" She laughed, trying to lighten the mood. She brushed the side of his hand with her pinkie. "I gave my mom a lot of grief about where I wanted to go to college. She couldn't afford it. I was determined not to end up like her. The day she died, I wasn't home. I knew how ill she was. I should have never left." An old, familiar guilt burned the backs of her eyes.

"Where were you?"

"In school. Taking finals." She twisted her lips and shrugged. "The memory still haunts me, but I'm honoring her memory by my research. To find a cure for the disease that claimed her life." She turned and studied his profile while he stared into the darkened yard. "I love my work. I get a lot of satisfaction from it." She nudged his arm. "You need to block out all the demands of everyone else and listen to the little voice inside you—your voice—and decide what God put you on the face of the earth to do. I've done a lot of praying about things. That was my mother's greatest gift. She taught me faith. My faith has kept me sane." She laughed. "*If* you think I'm sane."

He rolled his eyes and laughed. "It's all a matter of perspective, right?"

She reached over and covered his hand with hers. "You are truly blessed to have so many opportunities in life. Decide what you want to do. Pray on it."

He turned to face her. "The irony was never lost on me that my parents were missionaries and their own son lacks faith."

"It doesn't have to be that way." Her soft whisper blended with the crickets.

"Maybe," he said, noncommittally. He lifted his hand as if to caress her face, then seemed to think better of it, leaving Lily conflicted. Both relief and disappointment warmed her untouched cheeks. "Have you ever considered starting a family of your own? Slowing down a bit?"

Lily dragged her fingers along the smooth

railing. “A family? I’m not so sure about that, but I suppose I’ll eventually slow down. Do more things like working at the clinic. Do more things I want to do.”

James tilted his head. “I know something I want to do.” He took a step toward her, trapping her against the railing. He hooked a finger under her chin, lifting her face. Her heart beat wildly in her chest as he leaned in and brushed a kiss across her lips. He pulled back, a mischievous smile tipping the corners of his mouth. “I’ve wanted to do that for a very long time.”

Lily’s pink lips demanded he kiss them again, but he used tremendous restraint and resisted. She slipped past him and lifted her bottled water to her mouth, never taking her eyes from his.

“I wasn’t expecting that.” She gave him a serious look and angled her chin. “It was nice. Very nice.”

He laughed. “Why, thank you. Are you ever going to let me take you on a proper date?”

Lily’s eyes widened a fraction, but she didn’t say anything.

He rubbed a hand across his whiskered jaw. “Let’s see. What kind of things do you like to do on a date? I mean—” he internally shook his head “—where would you like me to take you?”

Lily bowed her head and picked at the label

on her water bottle. "I really appreciate everything you've done for me."

"Uh-oh. I know a brush-off when I hear it."

She held up a hand in protest. "It's not that. It's just that I never envisioned myself getting married, having kids. You know, the whole picket-fence thing."

"I wasn't proposing. I was asking you on a date." He watched ambiguous emotions play across her pretty features not for the first time that night.

A soft breeze kicked up. She hooked a strand of hair and dragged it away from her cheek. "You're such a great guy. I don't want to hurt you. Dating me would only lead to hurt."

"Pretty confident, aren't you?" He leaned in close, his pulse thumping in his ears, defying his calm-cool-collected facade. "What if I break *your* heart?"

Lily's eyes widened before she laughed. "This is the most bizarre conversation I've ever had. I like you, James. I really do, but I can't deal with any more complications in my life."

James scratched his forehead. "I've never met anyone as driven as you—except for me. It's almost like seeing myself from an objective position. Maybe I need to reexamine *my* priorities."

"Are you telling me I need to reexamine mine?" She looked at him skeptically.

"All work and no play makes Lily a very dull girl indeed." Amusement lit his eyes.

"This girl has too much work to do…and apparently a stalker to deal with." Lily giggled and covered her face. She then just as quickly pulled her hand away and forced a somber expression, then crumpled into a fit of giggles again. "I think I'm losing it. I'm cracking under all this pressure. Forget what I said earlier. I'm not sane." She brushed past him and stepped inside.

James let the breeze cool him off before he followed her inside. Watching her closely, he pulled out the chair across from hers at the small dinette.

"I'm sorry." She swiped a finger under her eyes. Planting her elbow on the table, she rested her chin in the palm of her hand.

"You're under a lot of pressure. And I'm sorry about the kiss out there. I got a little caught up in the moment." Well, he was only sorry it made her uncomfortable. He crossed his arms on the table. "You looked so beautiful out there. Irresistible."

A light came into her eyes. "I've never had anyone apologize for kissing me. Not that I've kissed a lot of guys…I mean." She waved her hand, flustered. "You don't want to date me anyway. Work is my life."

He understood where she was coming from.

He had been pushing off his personal life for years. Growing up, he had hoped to marry and fill his house with a ton of kids—the simple dream of an only child. But when his parents died, his world turned inside out.

Suddenly feeling very brave, James reached across the table and drew her hand away from her face. "After losing my parents, my grandparents became reluctant guardians. They shipped me off to boarding school. It was a pretty lonely existence. It made me a very guarded person." He dragged his thumb across the soft palm of her hand. He angled his head to catch her eye. "Being around you makes me want to take a risk. Open my heart."

She pulled her hand away and he stared for a moment at the space it had occupied.

"What are you afraid of?"

Lily blinked slowly. "We want different things."

"I'm only asking for a date, Lily." He tried to keep his tone even. "Get to know each other."

Leaning back in her chair, she crossed her arms and seemed to smirk at him. "Why bother? My life is the lab. And you plan to reenlist. We have no future."

"I'm not asking you to quit your job. And I won't be in the army forever." He narrowed his gaze. "What gives? There's something bigger going on here."

"Okay, you want to know why I don't want to go on a date with you?" The chair scraped across the hardwood floor, and she stood and paced the small space, her hands flexing and relaxing.

He shifted sideways in his chair. "Talk to me, Lily." He lifted his hand to touch her, then let it fall to his side.

Pausing for a moment, she looked at him; something flashed in her eyes he couldn't quite name. She blinked a few times, as if snapping out of it, and started pacing again. "Shortly after Emily was diagnosed with the same disease that killed my mother, I was tested for the gene that carries the disease."

Dread welled up in his gut. He stood and took Lily's hand. He tried to pull her into an embrace, but she stiffened, lifted her hand, planted it against his chest and gave him a gentle shove. "Don't."

She covered her mouth. "I can't have children. Not without worrying they may get sick. Not without worrying I might die before I get to see them grow up."

The pain etched on her features crushed the air from his lungs. "But a treatment is on the horizon." With his index finger, he tilted her face to force her to look at him.

"You're the only person I've ever told."

James couldn't imagine the burden she carried. "Did you get a second opinion?"

Her eyes glossed over. "My sister passed the disease on to Emily."

James followed Lily to the couch. Placing her palms together, she pressed them between her knees. "Even if I never actually get the disease, can I have children knowing they might? Even if I find a treatment. Is it fair?" She stared straight ahead, not meeting his eyes. "The disease is so rare, hardly anyone has heard of it. Yet, in my family, it scored a clean sweep."

"You have to have faith. Isn't that what you keep telling me?" He hated how cliché he sounded.

"Trust me, I've tried. Sometimes even I can't dig deep enough to find the faith I need."

ELEVEN

Lily swiveled on her stool to face the lab door when her assistant Sarah breezed in. Sarah froze and gave her a *what's-wrong?* stare. "You do remember I had an exam today, right? That's why I wasn't in." She pointed to her desk. "I came in to grab something."

Lily nodded. She had remembered. Otherwise, she would have been alarmed if neither of her assistants had shown up for work during a time when a stalker was harassing her.

Sarah flicked a gaze toward Talia's workstation. "She still hasn't shown, huh?"

"You seem more angry than concerned." Lily studied Sarah's face.

"Aren't *you* angry? Who ditches work?" Sarah grabbed something from her lab-coat pocket and slipped it into her purse. "I know Talia's been here longer than I have, but I don't know if I can keep picking up the slack for her. I know she's disappointed she didn't get into the Ph.D. program, but she needs to learn to put on her big-girl pants and get back to work. Talia's smart. Other opportunities will come up."

Lily put down her pen and planted her feet on the floor, perched on the edge of the stool. She slipped her hands into the pockets of her lab coat. "Do you think that's why she's not here? Because she's upset about not getting into the Ph.D. program?"

"It's my best guess. I overheard her a few weeks ago grumbling about not being appreciated around here. Only lately did I put two and two together."

"I wrote her a strong letter of recommendation." Lily ran a hand across the back of her neck.

"Talia would have no way of knowing that. The letter was sealed, right?"

Lily nodded and sighed. "Did Talia mention anything about taking a trip? Maybe with her new boyfriend?"

Sarah scoffed. "She doesn't seem the type, does she?" Sarah scrunched up her nose.

"James and I stopped by Talia's and chatted with her mother. She said Talia was on a business trip. Do you know anything about that?"

Sarah threw up her hands, apparently determined to clear herself of any wrongdoing. "No, but Talia and I aren't that close. It doesn't sound right to me, though."

"I can't figure out why she didn't get into the Ph.D. program. She had good grades."

"Who knows? Maybe they accepted fewer students this year." Sarah shrugged. "Don't stress yourself about it."

"I'm worried Talia's having trouble dealing with the fact she didn't get into the graduate program." Guilt expanded in her chest. Lily had been so focused on the research, she hadn't reached out to Talia. She had noticed Talia had become more withdrawn and moody, but quite frankly, she hadn't wanted to deal with it. "I wish Talia would have talked to me. I would have gladly shared the letter I wrote. It might have made her feel better. I do value her work. And I value yours, Sarah."

"Thanks, Doc." Sarah smiled. "Academic people put too much pressure on themselves until they implode. The only time I ever saw Talia express any real emotion was when she thought I was trying to take credit for her work. Then her true colors came out." Sarah raised her eyebrows at the memory.

"It's understandable that someone would want credit for their own work."

"I was pointing out a flaw in her research. I wasn't trying to take credit for that." Sarah's eyes grew hard. “She didn’t have to go psycho on me.”

The memory of small, quiet Talia trembling—teetering on the brink of a meltdown—while she accused Sarah of documenting her findings flashed in Lily’s mind. It had blown over as quickly as it had blown up.

A small blip in an otherwise peaceful coexistence.

Lily rubbed her gritty eyes. Had Talia’s response been appropriate or had her anger shown her lack of maturity in handling her emotions?

Lily fingered a paper clip in her pocket. “I wish I could talk to her. Assure her that everything is going to be okay. She’s not answering her cell phone, either.”

Sarah gestured to the door with her thumb. A look of contrition softened her features. “I’ve got a hot date waiting for me. How about you, Doc?”

Hands still in her pockets, Lily pushed off the stool. “Do I have a hot date?”

Sarah laughed. “No. I meant, are you leaving? But hey, if you have a hot date, all the better.”

Lily scratched her head. “I’m afraid my social life is quite boring.” The memory of James’s soft kiss heated her cheeks.

The door made a sucking sound when Sarah opened it. “Talia will show up. Maybe on

Monday. Then she'll act all indignant as if we shouldn't have touched her stuff while she was gone."

"I hope so. It's been a few days. I thought she would have shown up by now."

"I'm sure she's fine." Sarah dragged out the word *fine.* "Probably trying to figure out her next step since she won't be going to graduate school. Night, Doc."

"Night." Lily stared at the door long after it had closed.

Lily rolled her stiff shoulders. It was time to go home. She sat back down and put her paperwork in order.

A soft knock on the door made her jump. James peeked through the window along the edge of the door and Lily leaned forward to hide her smile behind a curtain of hair.

Slowly, she got up, crossed over to the door and opened it. "Sorry, have you been waiting for me?" She should have known. She still didn't have her car back from the collision shop.

"I have news." James spoke faster than usual.

"News?" The periphery of her vision started to fade.

James's eyes flashed bright. "Good news." He reached out and squeezed her arm, his hand warm through her sleeve. "I got the blood work back from your niece."

Lily froze and held her breath. Anticipation charged her nerve endings. *Calm down.* He had said good news, right?

"I had the lab compare her recent blood work with blood work from last year after her recovery and there's been no change. She's still in remission." He leaned in close, a bold smile lighting his entire face.

She let her shoulders drop. *Thank You, Lord.* "Thank God."

"I have a few phone calls in to specialists in the Buffalo area. Emily needs to be under the regular care of a physician." He gave her arm one more reassuring squeeze before dropping his hand. Suddenly, she felt adrift, floating high on the best possible news.

Briefly, Lily closed her eyes and concentrated on her feet firmly planted on the floor. "That is the best news." Stretching up on her tiptoes, she kissed his cheek. He smelled clean, like soap and subtle aftershave. She settled down onto her heels and heat crept up her neck and cheeks. She spun around and busied herself with some papers on her desk. "Did you call my sister?"

"Not yet. I just received the lab report and thought we could tell your sister in person."

The enormity of her relief made Lily forget all her worries. *This* was all that mattered. "Yes, let's do that." She grabbed her purse from the bottom desk drawer and strode toward the door, then turned back around. "You don't know how happy this makes me." She slipped her lab coat off and flung it up on the hook. "This definitely calls for a celebration."

James reached the door first and gestured for her to go ahead of him. "Are you asking me out on a date?"

"Ha. No, but you can come with me to share the news." She couldn't help but smile at his good-natured ribbing.

"Sounds great. I'll take what I can get. Let's go."

"What sounds great?" Kara stood in the hall with her arms crossed over her chest. She smiled coyly at them. "Going on a date?"

Lily narrowed her gaze, wondering if all her coworkers were conspiring to set her up on a date. She ran a hand down her blouse. Did she seem that desperate? It didn't matter. Nothing could dull her joy today. "We received some great news about my niece, Emily."

"That's wonderful." The lilt in Kara's voice seemed forced, considering the tightness around her eyes and brows. She looked stressed.

Lily did a double take at her friend. "Everything okay?"

"Oh, yeah, you know me. Running around like

a crazy person for Mrs. O'Reilly." She tipped her head to see around Lily to James. "No offense."

James held up a hand. "None taken."

"She has you running around on a Friday night?" Lily glanced down the long corridor, anxious to share the news with her sister.

"I have to take care of a few things at the travel agent for the O'Reillys' cruise." Kara dug into her purse and pulled out her keys. "I just wandered down to this remote part of the complex to see if you needed a ride."

"She's all set," James said. "We're heading out."

Kara's mouth formed a perfectly round O. She leaned in close. "Didn't realize you and the good doctor were a thing."

"We're not." Fiddling with the clasp on her purse, Lily tried to keep her tone even. "It's better if I use the buddy system."

"Good idea," Kara said. "Well, I better go." She jangled the keys in her hand. "I have lots to do. I need to start looking for a new job."

Lily grabbed her friend's hand. "What?"

"Well, you don't think Mrs. O'Reilly needs me when they're traveling around the world?"

"Did she tell you that?"

"She told me my hours would be reduced."

Kara tucked a strand of hair behind her ear. "But I can see the writing on the wall."

"Oh, I'm sorry." Lily glanced over her shoulder at James, then back at her friend. "Are you okay?"

Waving her hand in dismissal, Kara smiled. "Oh, listen to me. I didn't mean to be a killjoy. Don't let me hold you up."

Lily caught her friend's eye.

"Really, I'm okay," Kara insisted. "Go."

James watched Lily kneel next to her niece, Emily, who worked a puzzle on the coffee table. Bethany sat on the edge of a blue recliner with a worried expression in her eyes.

"It must be bad, right?" Bethany wrung her hands, her voice barely above a whisper. "You wouldn't take the time to come here if it wasn't bad."

James reached over and touched Bethany's shoulder. "It's good news. We didn't mean to worry you."

"It's wonderful news." Lily spoke up, smoothing a hand down her niece's long hair before pressing a kiss to her forehead. The scene tugged at James's heart. Smiling, she glanced up at James with bright eyes. "Emily's still in remission."

"But her symptoms?" Bethany's eyes grew

wide and a tear spilled down her cheek. Emily stopped working the puzzle and stared at her mother, no doubt wondering why her mom was crying.

"Everything's okay, Emily. Your mom's happy," James said, wanting to reassure her.

Bethany swatted at her wet cheeks and smiled. "Yes, honey, everything's fine." Her daughter lifted another puzzle piece and tried to fit it into a section near the corner. One blue piece looked like the next, but the young girl was determined. "So she probably had a twenty-four-hour flu or something?"

"Yes, most likely." Lily pointed to another section of the puzzle and Emily snapped in her piece. Lily touched the young girl's hand. "How do you feel today?"

"Fine, Aunt Lily." Bored with the puzzle, Emily scooted away from her and stood by the fan in the window. "I'm sweaty."

Bethany laughed. Another tear tracked down her cheek. "We don't have AC," she said to James, by way of apology. Then she lowered her voice. "Are you sure the symptoms don't mean something more?" She kept her voice low, but Emily was preoccupied with humming into the fan. The air swept back Emily's hair from her cheeks and forehead.

"Yes," James said. "You'll have to stay on top

of things. From now on, no more skipping doctor's appointments." He dug a business card out of his pocket. "This physician is the best when it comes to genetic diseases. He agreed to see Emily."

Bethany opened her mouth to say something and Lily jumped in. "We'll figure out the details of the insurance. Don't worry about it."

"Thank you," Bethany said. "This has been an answer to my prayers."

A long-forgotten memory of his mother sitting on his bed in a rustic setting in some foreign land niggled at the back of his brain. No matter how busy his mother was, she always tucked him in and helped him say his bedtime prayers. She claimed their work needed lots of prayers. That she and his father didn't know all the answers…

"Mom," Emily whined, snapping James out of his reverie. "It's so hot in here. I wish I could go swimming." Emily flopped on her mother's lap in a dramatic fashion.

Bethany ran a hand down her daughter's long hair. "I already told you the town pool closed at five."

"Hey," James said, suddenly getting an idea, "if it's okay with your mom, maybe we can pick up a pizza and head back to my grandparents' house and swim."

Emily bolted upright. "Can we, Mom?"

An uncertain expression flitted across Bethany's face. She glanced over at her daughter, then her sister, then back at James. "If we wouldn't be imposing."

"Not at all. My grandparents have that beautiful pool and no one uses it." He met Lily's gaze, guessing he should have cleared it with her first, but her demeanor suggested nothing could bother her tonight. Not after the wonderful news regarding Emily's health.

"Can we?" Emily jumped up and down.

"How does that sound to you, Lily?" Bethany asked.

"It sounds like a perfect summer evening."

Emily continued her dramatics. She climbed up on her mother's lap and fanned herself. "It sounds awesome to me because I am boil-*ling*."

"You're making me hot." Bethany playfully pushed Emily from her lap. "Let's get your bathing suit on." James pulled out his cell phone. "I'll order a pizza and have it delivered to the house."

Planting her hands on the coffee table, Lily pushed up from her knees. A slow smile spread across her beautiful face. He narrowed his gaze as she leaned in close and brushed a soft kiss across his cheek. "Thanks. My sister and niece can really use this."

He could smell the fresh scent of her shampoo. He studied her expression for a moment before snapping out of it. "You're welcome." He tipped his head toward the front door. "Let's get moving before we all melt in here."

"Go ahead. We'll be down in a minute," Bethany called from the other room.

James guided Lily outside with a hand to the small of her back. When he climbed into his side of the vehicle, he looked across at Lily, who seemed more content than he'd seen her in a long time.

"Was today a good day?" he asked, already knowing the answer.

Her pink lips curved into a smile that crinkled the corners of her eyes. "Definitely. A very good day."

The trill of Lily's phone disturbed the mood. "Sorry." She bent over her purse and fished around for her phone.

Lily answered it and her features grew pinched. After a moment she said, "Are you sure, Mrs. York? Here, I'm going to put you on speakerphone. James O'Reilly is with me."

Lily pulled the phone away from her ear and hit the speaker button. "...don't care much for those fancy things. Hello, can you hear me?" Mrs. York's harsh voice filled the interior of the car.

"Yes, Mrs. York. Tell James what you just told me." All the color had drained from Lily's face.

"Well, Dr. O'Reilly, that guy that's been all over the news… I think that's the guy my Talia brought home." She hacked violently. After she regained her composure she said, "My Talia's book smart, but she's never been much for common sense. Never been much a good judge of character."

"Mrs. York," Lily said, "that composite was on the news the night we came to see you. How come you're only calling us now?"

Mrs. York harrumphed, as if she had been offended. "My eyes aren't so good. I didn't see the resemblance till I got up close to the TV."

Lily could imagine the older woman shaking her head.

"I think it's him. I got a good look at him in person when he visited my Talia. We both had to go around a stack of newspapers. He nearly kicked my walker out from under me, he was in such a hurry."

"What's his name, Mrs. York?" James spoke up.

"Frank. That's all I know."

"Mrs. York, have you seen Talia lately?" James leaned closer to the phone, his shoulder brushing against Lily's. Across the courtyard, he noticed Bethany locking the main door to her apartment. Emily skipped around a light pole, a beach towel dangling from her hand.

"No, Talia hasn't come back from her business trip." Mrs. York sounded a little miffed. "Don't you people keep track of these things?"

James and Lily locked eyes. Into the phone he said, "Thanks for letting us know." He cleared his throat. "Do you need anything while Talia's away?"

Silence stretched over the line for a moment. "My Talia always takes care of everything. She'll take care of me when she gets home."

If she gets home.

TWELVE

"This is wonderful." Bethany lounged at the pool steps, swooshing her foot in circles, sloshing the water around. "It's great to get out of the apartment. I've been imagining the worst about Emily's health for days. A huge weight has been lifted."

"I'm so thankful Emily's okay."

"I don't think I stopped praying since Emily had her blood drawn." Bethany gathered her hair and twisted it into a messy bun. "I guess I should have trusted God more. I would have saved myself the worry."

"I think worrying runs in the family." Lily smiled, tilting her face toward the warm evening sun. Rolling her shoulders, she couldn't get Mrs. York's phone call out of her mind. She had to be mistaken. What would Talia be doing with the man who'd been stalking her? Maybe Mrs. York hadn't seen the composite clearly. Her vision was failing. Perhaps a lonely old woman had let her imagination get the best of her.

A loud squeal came from the other end of the pool. James was doing laps with Emily—the short width of the pool—his powerful arms cutting through the water. He'd stop at each side and wait for Emily to catch up, then he'd give her a head start to the other side, pretending to fall behind and at the last minute beating her to the edge of the pool. Emily's giggle made all seem right with the world. At least for now.

Lily rolled up the hems of her pants and stepped down onto the first step. *Enjoy the moment. Clear your mind for right now. This moment.* The water enveloped her feet and ankles. *Ah.* She playfully kicked, splashing her sister. Bethany threw up her arms, but defending herself against the large drops of water was useless.

"Knock it off before I pull you in." The spark in Bethany's eyes belied her menacing grimace. She reached up and yanked on Lily's wrist.

"Oh, no, you don't." Lily grabbed on to the silver railing to anchor herself. Her sister released her wrist as quickly as she had grabbed on.

"Ah, you're too gullible. You really think I'd toss my smarty-pants sister into the water?"

"Good to know my brain power holds some sway." Clutching the railing, Lily lowered herself onto the edge of the pool, watching her sister's hands for any sudden movements.

Bethany leaned over and playfully bumped Lily's shoulder with her own. "I'm so glad we've become friends." She dipped her head and smiled shyly. "I'm sorry it took Emily getting sick a couple years ago for me and you to reconnect." She tucked a loose strand of hair behind her ear. "I wasn't the best big sister when we were growing up, was I?"

Lily mimicked the gesture and nudged her sister's shoulder right back. "I imagine I was a pest, too. I succeeded in my job as your little sister." They'd had their share of battles growing up in a small duplex with a single mother. They must have driven her crazy.

Bethany leaned back, bracing herself on straightened arms. "This is nice. I wish the summers weren't so short."

Lily twirled her foot in the water. "This feels like bathwater."

Bethany tipped her head toward the mansion behind them. "I guess they can afford to heat the pool. The town pool is absolutely freezing. Like ice cubes. Emily's lips are always purple when she gets out."

"Oh, I remember that. As a kid, I always thought I hated swimming. Turns out I only hated cold water." Lily laughed. "Remember riding our bikes to the pool when Mom was at work?"

"You'd bug me until I took you." Bethany swished her fingers in the water and flicked them at Lily. Dark spots marred the thighs of her khaki pants. "Come to think of it, I *did* think you were a little pest."

"I suppose it's hard having a sister six years younger who follows you around."

Bethany leaned forward, resting her elbows on her knees. "Now who needs who? I am so blessed to have you as a sister." She turned to face Lily. "Sorry I treated you like a bother. I don't know what I'd do without you." She lowered her voice. "I don't know what Emily would do…or what I'd do without my daughter. She's my heart."

Lily reached down, scooped a handful of water and let it flow through her fingers. The news today that Emily was in remission was a reminder of how truly blessed they were. Her gaze drifted to the bubbling fountain at the edge of the pool. A person could get used to living like this. "This is nice."

"I'm sure you don't do this enough." Bethany watched James and Emily at the other side of the pool. "You really should take time for yourself."

A high-pitched squeal sounded from the deep

end. James had lifted Emily and tossed her toward the shallow end. Her niece made a big splash, spun around and swam back to James, a huge smile on her narrow face. Emily wrapped her small hands around his neck and hung on. "Throw me again, Dr. James."

Bethany whispered, "He's really good with kids."

Lily swooshed her fingers in the warm water. An emptiness stretched inside her. He'd make a great dad someday. "He's great with the patients at the clinic, too."

"So he's giving up practicing medicine to run Medlink?"

"His grandfather wants to retire." Lily purposely gave an evasive answer. James really planned to reenlist, but she supposed that was his news to share.

Bethany nodded, her attention focused on her daughter. Grabbing the railing, she pulled herself up, gesturing with her free hand to Emily. "Give Dr. James a break. His arms are going to fall off if he has to throw you one more time."

"It's okay," Emily hollered. "He likes it."

Slowly shaking her head, Bethany sat back down.

"It's fine. I think I still have one good arm," James called across the pool. "One. Good. Arm."

He hooked his arm and dragged Emily farther into the deep end.

Lily winced, unable to believe such a little kid could emit such an ear-piercing squeal.

Bethany shifted toward Lily, an expectant look on her face. "So…what's going on between you two? You seem to be spending a lot of time together. Is it serious?" The barrage of questions made Lily uncomfortable. Or maybe her line of questioning had struck too close to home.

"Nothing's going on." Nothing in the relationship department, anyway. Or was she lying to herself? "We have a lot of business-related things going on right now." Lily hoped her sister couldn't detect the evasiveness in her voice. She hadn't told her sister about her stalker, either. Bethany didn't watch much TV, and she refused to watch the news since, in her sister's words, it was only *bad* news. Bethany had enough on her mind, between her daughter's health and her employment status.

"I'm not buying it. You guys would make a great couple."

Lily laughed. "Why? Because we're both physicians?" She did her best to sound flippant and figured she had failed miserably.

Bethany tucked her chin and raised her eyebrows. "Do I really need to spell it out for you?"

Lily waved her hands. "No, please don't." She lowered her voice to a whisper. "We're just friends."

Bethany narrowed her gaze. "Why are you staying at the carriage house? You love your cottage."

"How did you know I was staying here?"

"So it's true." Bethany's eyes widened. "I thought I heard Edna mention something to you when we came in."

She swooshed her foot in the water, debating how much to tell her sister. "Someone left a dead rat on my porch at the cottage. I'll feel safer here until the police track this guy down."

Bethany jerked back and her nose turned up in disgust. "Oh, no! That's creepy. Why do you suppose someone did that?"

Lily flicked a gaze toward James, who was in a *how-long-can-you-hold-your-breath* contest with her niece. "Chief Farley's investigating."

Bethany cut her a sideways glance, obviously not buying her answer. "We're going to chat. Later." She crossed her arms. "So you're telling me you and James aren't an item? You should seriously reconsider." Bethany fluttered her feet in the water. "I can't remember the last time you had a serious boyfriend."

Before Emily got sick, Lily had dated casually. After Emily got sick, she didn't have time to spare. But a treatment was now at her fingertips.

"I don't ever plan on getting married or having children. I..." Bowing her head, Lily ran a hand across her mouth, realizing she didn't want to have this conversation. Not with her sister.

Bethany's features grew slack in disbelief. "Wait. Don't tell me you're never going to have children because you're afraid they'll get sick."

Lily pressed her fist to her mouth, as if she were holding her words back.

Bethany sat up ramrod straight. "I'd do anything to make my daughter completely healthy, but I never regret having her."

Lily reached out and grabbed her sister's hand. "Oh, that's not what I meant at all. You didn't know you carried the gene before you got pregnant. I know I carry the gene. I can't have children knowing they could be sick. Even with a treatment. I'm afraid to take the chance."

Bethany blinked a few times, as if processing the information. "I didn't know...." She shook her head. Cold anger sparked in her eyes. "I'm sorry you carry the gene. But you can't live your life afraid of everything."

"We've both experienced so much loss. I never thought I'd get over losing Mom." Lily studied her sister's face, aware of James and Emily playing on the other side of the pool. "If

I'm truly honest, I *am* afraid." Lily shrugged. "I can't help it."

"I pray every day God will guide you in your research. But I've also made peace with the fact that God may have other plans. I learned a long time ago that I have to live in the moment. Thank God for the blessings I have. The ones I have right now." Bethany tapped the stamped concrete adamantly with her index finger for emphasis.

Bethany stood and walked to the deep end. She crouched by the side of the pool and stretched out her hand. "Come here, little mermaid."

Emily sucked in a huge breath and disappeared under the surface. She popped up and grabbed the side of the pool near her mother. Bethany leaned over and planted a kiss on her daughter's wet hair. "Aren't you getting tired?"

Emily shook her head, her wet ponytail flinging from side to side.

"A few more minutes, then come out for a little break." A trace of concern lined her sister's face. Emily had been sick only a few days earlier.

"Pizza's here." Edna strode toward them, carrying two boxes of pizza.

Lily stood. "Thanks, Edna. Where are the paper plates? I'll go get them."

Edna shook her head. "Charlie's bringing

everything you need. Sit. Relax." She leaned in close and whispered, "It's nice to see you enjoying time with your family and James." The older woman hitched a knowing eyebrow. Apparently, they were all conspiring against her.

Instead of arguing, Lily simply said, "Thank you."

Charlie appeared a second later holding plates, cups and a bottle of soda. Placing them on the table, he scanned the pool. "Nice to see someone using the pool. Do you know how much time I put into keeping it clean? I think you guys are the first ones to use it this summer." His smile revealed white teeth against a suntanned face.

Lily patted his arm. "It's refreshing."

James climbed out of the pool and wrapped a towel around his shoulders. He walked by Emily and tweaked her nose. "I want an underwater rematch. I know I can hold my breath longer."

Emily giggled. "Nope. I can hold *my* breath longer."

James jutted out his chin. "We'll see." He reached across Lily and grabbed a piece of pepperoni pizza. "Yum. All that swimming made me hungry." He handed the plate to Emily, then got one for himself. The four of them sat around the glass table, Emily happily chatting away. James looked up from his pizza and caught Lily's eye.

Warmth blossomed in her chest. Could she let down her guard for this man? She pulled a cup from the top of the stack and poured Emily a little soda. Why did it matter? He was planning to reenlist.

Gone from her life.

James was surprised to see Emily polish off two pieces of pizza. The adults chatted and Emily's head started to bob as she fought the good fight to keep her eyes open.

James tipped his head toward his swimming buddy. "Looks like Emily wore herself out."

Her mother laughed. "Oh, she's going to be grumpy. I better get going."

"I'll drive you home whenever you're ready," James said, truly sorry to see the evening come to an end.

"Dr. James, I'm heading into town to pick up a few things at the hardware store. I can drive Miss Bethany and Emily home." Charles had returned to the pool area to replace the liner in the garbage can.

James glanced at Bethany. Her eyes brightened. "That would be great, as long as you don't mind," she said. "This way James and Lily can sit and enjoy the evening."

Out of the corner of his eye, he thought he saw

Lily give her sister the stink eye. He refrained from laughing out loud.

Taking Emily's hand, Bethany nudged her out of the chair. Emily groaned a little as they headed to the pool house to put on dry clothes.

James stood, gathered the plates and napkins and tossed them in the garbage bag Charlie was holding. "I appreciate your driving them home."

"My pleasure, Dr. James." Charlie tied up the bag. "I have to get a few things out of my car, but I'll be ready whenever they are."

James sat back down at the table. "You're awfully quiet." He tried to read the expression in Lily's beautiful brown eyes.

"Tired, I guess." She seemed to mentally shake herself. "I had a great time tonight. It's what I needed." She dragged her hand over her long ponytail. "It's what my sister and Emily needed, too."

"Well, then we'll have to do it more often."

Lily looked down at her thumbnail, then slowly lifted her eyes to meet his. "Maybe it's not such a great idea if we spend so much time together."

"So you didn't enjoy this evening?" He forced a light and teasing tone despite the wet blanket she had tossed over his good mood.

"I had a great time. I love to hear Emily laugh."

He studied her closely. "I love to hear *you* laugh."

Lily's cheeks turned a soft shade of pink. "You're relentless."

"Can you blame me?" He pressed his tongue into his cheek.

He followed her gaze to the pool house. No sign of her sister and niece. "I really enjoy hanging out with you, too. But it doesn't make sense. We've been over this. You plan on reenlisting. I'm busy in the lab."

Resting his elbows on his thighs, he reached out and captured her hand. "Let's take one day at a time." He tipped his head, hoping she'd look up at him. "I just know we could have something great." He playfully tugged on one of her fingers. "Why can't we enjoy the time we have?"

Lily closed her eyes briefly, her long lashes brushing against her smooth skin. A myriad of emotions flitted across her face. "Because it will only hurt that much more when you do have to leave."

He exhaled sharply and leaned back in the chair. "Wow. I wasn't expecting that."

A tired smile lifted the corners of her lips. "Honesty, right?"

His mind whirled. A part of him felt like a teenager, trying to figure out what to say next.

"Excuse me, Dr. James." It was Edna.

"Yes?" Disappointment flooded his system. He wanted to sit here and talk to Lily more. Get into her heart and mind.

"Your grandfather would like to see you in the great room."

"Thanks, Edna. I'll be right in." Watching Edna walk back toward the house, he paused a moment. When it became clear to him Lily wasn't going to say anything more, he stood. Emily and Bethany emerged from the pool house all smiles.

Forcing a smile of his own, he waved to them. "Charlie will take you home whenever you're ready."

"Thanks," Bethany said. Lily nodded without saying anything.

James threw on his T-shirt, then followed the path to the house.

"Hi, James." His grandfather stood in the center of the room leaning heavily on his cane.

"Grandfather."

The older gentleman gave him a curt nod. Turning, he shuffled toward a wingback chair and sat down. He gestured with an open palm to the matching one. He hung his cane over the arm of the chair.

"If you don't mind, I'll stand. My swim trunks are wet."

His grandfather tipped his head toward the

pool. "I see. You and Lily are spending a lot of time together." He lifted a bushy eyebrow. "Maybe it's time to settle down."

"Are you spending too much time with Grandmother? You sound like her."

His brows snapped together. "I think you're right. Since when did I care about those kinds of things? My focus has always been on work." His voice grew quiet. "Although, when you get old, you start to focus on what's important. Family. Children. Those things are what are important."

"Is that what you called me in to talk about?" James shifted his weight.

"No, but I know how much you love when your grandmother asks those questions. Since she's off at a garden party..." He let his words trail off.

"Thanks." The single word sounded droll.

"I'm worried."

The sudden shift in topics made James narrow his gaze. His grandfather never spoke this way. "What's going on?"

"The board of directors is calling a meeting for Monday morning. They see some discrepancies in the accounting."

"Is there an explanation?" James's gaze drifted around the room with all its expensive works of art and furnishings. His stomach twisted. No, his grandfather was a ruthless businessman, but he was an honest one.

A muscle ticked in his grandfather's jaw.

His grandfather planted his hands on the arms of the chair and pushed himself to a standing position. "I built Medlink up to what it is today."

"Have you had a chance to look at the books yourself?"

His grandfather visibly paled. He shook his head. His arm trembled as he supported his weight on the cane. "The board is looking into it." His voice grew quieter as he moved toward the foyer. "I'm confident this is a misunderstanding."

"Are you?" James's throat felt parched.

His grandfather turned around. His eyes grew hard. "It has to be a misunderstanding." He placed his hand on the banister and bowed his head. "I'm afraid my health has kept me out of the office more than I would have liked this past year."

James ran those words over and over in his head.

His grandfather pointed to the French doors. "We'll talk more later. I'll let you get back to your company."

James wanted to ask a million questions but decided they'd have to wait.

His grandfather slowly climbed the stairs.

James stepped onto the back patio, a little stunned. He was relieved to get some fresh air. He found Emily and Bethany sitting by the pool, but the chair where Lily had been sitting was empty.

"Where's Lily?" He had a heightened awareness of his surroundings, just like he had when he had traveled into unfriendly territory while in the army. But it made no sense. He knew she was safe here. They had installed extra security precautions.

"Edna and Charlie had some groceries for her." Bethany stood, gathered her bags and tossed her towel over her shoulder. "Thank you for having us, James. We really enjoyed it."

Emily smiled up at him. "I had so much fun, Dr. James."

He crouched down. "Well, I'm glad. We'll have to do it again soon."

"Don't leave," Lily hollered from the top landing of the stairs leading to her second-story apartment in the carriage house. Gliding her hand along the railing, she jogged down the stairs to her sister. She drew Emily into a big hug. "I'll see you soon, okay?"

Emily's eyes lit up. "Can we come over swimming again soon, Mom?"

"Oh, I don't…" Bethany stammered.

James jumped in. "Absolutely. We'll make

plans soon." His gaze met Lily's and she gave him a sad smile. This woman was going to be his undoing. Why did things have to be so complicated?

"Thanks very much, Dr. James. I had a lot of fun."

James ruffled her wet hair, leaving it sticking up at awkward angles. "I had fun, too. Now, let me walk you out front."

Lily jerked her thumb toward the carriage house. "There are a few more things in Edna's kitchen I need to bring up to my apartment. I really should help her."

"Wait a few minutes and I can help," James offered.

Lily held up her palms. "No, really, I'm fine." She turned on her heel and jogged toward Edna's door. "Night," she hollered over her shoulder.

James stared after her, the warm glow of the evening quickly dissolving.

"You really shouldn't have." Lily slid the last box of fresh produce and groceries off Edna's kitchen counter in the apartment below hers.

Edna waved her hand. "You have to eat. Stay healthy. You work too much." Her friendly smile revealed crooked teeth. "It's so nice to see you having fun with your family and Dr. James."

"My niece needed a change of pace."

A twinkle lit Edna's eyes. "So your niece is okay?"

"Yes, she is. Thank you." Lily adjusted her hands on the cumbersome cardboard box and rested it on the corner of the island.

Charlie walked through the door, planted a kiss on his wife's plump cheek and draped his arm over her shoulder. "Edna loves having you around to fuss over." A twinge of pink colored the older woman's cheeks.

"She's too kind to me." Lily smiled at the easy display of affection between the older couple. Raised as the daughter of a single mother, Lily had never witnessed firsthand what true love looked like.

Edna patted her husband's hand resting on her shoulder, then slipped out from under his touch. "One can never be too kind." She tucked a strand of Lily's hair behind her ear. "It reminds me of the summers during college when you lived here. How I enjoyed having you around. I never had children of my own."

A ribbon of nostalgia tightened around Lily's heart. "I was lucky to have you around. It felt like home when everything else in my world seemed adrift."

Edna tapped Lily's cheek gently with the palm of her hand. "You've done well. Your mother would be proud. Don't be so hard on yourself. Allow yourself to be happy."

"Easier said than done." She patted Edna's work-worn hand. "Thanks again for this." She hoisted the box, then balanced it on her hip.

Charlie hustled toward her. "Let me take that upstairs for you."

"Oh, no, I'm fine. You're already doing me a big favor driving my sister and niece home." Lily smiled.

Charlie scooped the car keys off the counter. "The little one wanted to make a quick pit stop before we hit the road. They should be ready now." He kissed Edna on the cheek again. "Be back soon." Charlie went ahead of Lily and held the door.

"Good night, dear," Edna called from inside the house.

Balancing the box in her arms in front of her, Lily negotiated the stairs hugging the exterior of the little carriage house. When she had first laid eyes on this quaint carriage house all those years ago, it amazed her that it was tucked in behind the main house. She would have loved to grow up here instead of the cramped duplex her mother could barely afford. Guilt slammed into her. Her mother had worked hard to provide for her two daughters after their father chose booze over family. Her mother had done the best she could.

At the top of the stairs, she balanced the box on her knee and pushed open the door. She had kept it slightly ajar from her last trip up the stairs. Her apartment was a smaller version of Edna and Charlie's apartment downstairs. It was cozy.

She slid the box along the surface of the island counter. She spun around and opened the fridge to put away the groceries.

"I'm so sorry." A disembodied voice floated to her from the other side of the open refrigerator door. Pinpricks of terror rained down over her skin as she froze midmotion with her hand on the refrigerator door. Her mind whirled with the possibilities. Slowly, she closed the refrigerator door, her heart lodged in her throat.

Talia stood there, her straggly blond hair in need of a comb, her eyes wide, mirroring Lily's fear.

All Lily's instincts screamed for her to remain calm. "Talia? What are you doing here? How did you get onto the property?" The vacant look in her lab assistant's eyes made Lily's knees grow weak. She decided to change her approach. "We've all been worried about you." She kept her voice calm—even—carefully selecting her words. She flicked a gaze toward the door.

"I didn't know." The corners of Talia's mouth pulled down, making her look much older than her twenty-some years.

Lily took a step toward the door she had left unsecured when she ran downstairs to see her family off. Her fingertips tingled. Mentally she scolded herself. How could she have been so careless after everything that'd been going on? She was supposed to be safe on the O'Reilly property. The wrought-iron gate to the backyard had a key-code entry. Yet Talia had made it unseen into her apartment.

Tiny dots danced in Lily's line of vision.

Talia looked like a scared rabbit and Lily didn't want to test her limits by making any sudden movements. She lowered her voice. "What didn't you know, Talia?" The words scratched out of her parched mouth. The spike of adrenaline made her dizzy. She feared she was going to pass out.

"The man who attacked you at the clinic. I saw his photo on the news." With a crazy look in her eyes, Talia stepped toward Lily. Lily backed up and bumped into the fridge with the back of her heel. The younger woman's hand shot out and grabbed Lily's upper arm. Her fingers were incredibly cold despite the balmy night, her grip surprisingly strong.

"Let go of my arm." Lily stayed composed

despite the adrenaline surging through her veins. "You're scaring me."

"I thought he liked me. But he tricked me…." Talia's pupils were huge, black holes. She slid her gaze to where her fingers dug into Lily's arm. Confusion haunted the depths of her eyes. Talia eased her grip. Her face crumpled in anguish. "He told me he loved me."

Lily glanced toward the door, then back at Talia. Mrs. York's phone call came to mind. "What's his name?"

"Frank Smith."

"You didn't do anything wrong. You didn't know." Lily watched Talia's expression soften, giving Lily hope she was saying the right thing. *Please guide me, Lord.*

Talia ran a shaky hand through her scraggly hair. "He convinced me to take a little vacation with him. He told me I deserved it after how you treated me. He told me I should skip work. Show you how much you really needed me."

"I don't understand."

Red rimmed Talia's eyes. "I worked so hard. All I needed was a strong letter of recommendation." Her eyes grew dark. "Because of you…"

Lily shook her head. "I wrote a wonderful letter of recommendation." She hated how her voice shook. "I can show you. On my laptop."

"Really?" Talia's lips quivered. "No, I don't

believe you. When I complained to Frank about not getting into the program, he asked me a lot of questions. *He* was the one who figured out it *had* to have been *your* letter that ruined my chances."

"No, it couldn't have been. He was manipulating you." Lily reached out, but stopped short of touching her employee's arm.

"No, that can't be true." Talia's face crumpled. "I'm so stupid. I can't figure out what's going on. But Frank told me I was in as deep as he was."

"Why?" Tiny pinpricks blanketed Lily's scalp. "What did you do?"

"I brought him into the lab." Her eyes ping-ponged around the small space. "He just acted like he belonged and came through security right behind me." Her nose flared, and a stream of snot ran into her mouth. "I never had such a good-looking boyfriend. I loved the attention."

"Why did you bring him into the lab?" All the colors in the room grew vivid and distinct, disorienting.

What had Talia done?

"He said he wanted to see where I worked. But after his photo was broadcast all over the news, he told me to keep quiet or he'd tell everyone I stole the research files on Regen."

"This Frank, he has my research files?" Lily's voice climbed an octave. Her limbs went to jelly.

Talia nodded. "The computer files."

"Why, Talia? Why?"

"I didn't know he had them. Not until today. He told me I had to be quiet. Told me I'd be blamed. He was the one who planted the rat in my bedroom closet. He wanted you to think I killed the rat and left it on your porch." Talia bowed her head, then lifted it suddenly with a fierce determination in her eyes. "I snuck out after he passed out from drinking. I have to go." She pushed Lily against the refrigerator. Lily cracked her elbow on the stainless-steel door. The young woman bolted toward the exit, her stringy hair flying behind her. Fear—for Talia—swept over Lily. The look of desperation in Talia's eyes took Lily's breath away.

"Wait. Don't go. It'll be okay. I'll help you get this straightened out."

A horrifying cry erupted from the girl's mouth. Talia hit the edge of the open door hard with an *oomph*. Groaning, she bounced off, shifted and darted outside. The sound of feet on metal stairs sounded like tiny explosions in the night air.

Lily raced toward the open door. "Wait, Talia. We can fix this." She leaned over the railing and yelled at Talia as she ran toward the thick landscaping edging the deepest part of the yard.

Spinning on the balls of her feet, Lily turned

and raced down the stairs. She had to stop Talia. A flash of blue caught her eye. James jogged down the path toward her, fear in his eyes. Lily stopped short and pressed a hand to her chest. "You scared me."

"Are you all right?"

"Yes." Lily pointed frantically toward the back of the deep yard. "It's Talia. We have to stop her."

"Talia? Where?"

Lily pointed and James took off running. She followed him, but was slowed when she stepped on something sharp. A quick examination of her foot told her nothing was bleeding. Resuming her pursuit, she caught sight of James emerging from the thick foliage at the edge of the property. He swatted at unseen insects.

"Where did she go?"

James shook his head. "My guess? Through the large gap in the chain-link fence." He glanced at a deep cut on his arm. "I couldn't fit through, but I have no doubt that's how Talia made her escape."

THIRTEEN

Lily sat on the couch in the great room of O'Reilly Manor twisting her hands in her lap. Fingers smoothing the Band-Aid over his recent injury, James sat on the arm of the couch, resisting the urge to run his hand across Lily's back. The last time he had seen her so frail was shortly after her mother had died, when she had moved into the carriage house. He'd hardly known her back then. They had crossed paths only on the rare occasion when she had accompanied her mother to work. At the time of her mother's death, he'd been only twenty himself and still raw from his parents' deaths five years earlier. The grief he saw in her mirrored the emptiness haunting his soul.

"We have a real problem here," his grandfather said, leaning forward in his chair, resting his crossed wrists on his cane, his hair disheveled as if they had disturbed his sleep. He wore a brown robe, tied at the waist, and striped pajama bottoms.

"Security's on it." Striding back into the room, Stephanie dropped her cell phone into her oversize designer bag. Her long blond hair was pulled into a high ponytail and she was perfectly made up. Apparently, she had just gotten home from a date when James had called her to come by their grandparents' house.

"I don't understand," Stephanie said. "I thought we had increased security after the nightmare during Grandfather's party." She plopped her purse onto the coffee table and let out a heavy sigh. "That deranged girl should have never had access to the property." Stephanie seemed disproportionately annoyed, as if *she* had been attacked.

His grandmother strolled into the room, looking almost regal in her silky nightclothes. "This really could have waited until morning." She rested her hand on his grandfather's shoulder. "He needs his sleep."

His grandfather waved her off, lifting his cane as if he were shooing a pesky ankle biter. "I need to return to work full-time. Everything's falling apart."

His grandmother brushed a kiss across her husband's cheek. "You promised me you'd take it easy."

He pushed to his feet and jabbed his cane in Stephanie's direction, barely missing her shin. "*I* already talked to the head of Security."

Stephanie narrowed her gaze and flicked her fingers toward her purse. "Now we both called." She lifted a perfectly groomed eyebrow, as if issuing a challenge. But something in her gaze, a shadow of doubt, unease perhaps, had James watching her closely.

"That's not important right now," his grandfather said, a perturbed expression on his wrinkled features. "Go on, James. What were you saying?"

James stood. "Security assumed the intruder last weekend gained access through the unlocked main gate. They had no reason to suspect someone had cut through the fence. The breach is hidden by some shrubbery on both sides of the fence."

"What do we pay these guys for?" Stephanie asked, disgust dripping from her voice. She spun around and glared at Lily. "Now, what did your lab assistant—what's her name, Talia?—say to you?"

Lily rested an elbow on the arm of the couch and explained how Talia had recognized the man on the news as the man she'd been dating, a man named Frank Smith. When Talia had confronted him, he had told her if she came forward, he'd tell everyone she gave him the research files on Regen. Lily shuddered and her elbow slipped off the arm of the couch. "Talia claims that if he does have the notes, he stole them. She naively let him into the lab."

Stephanie gasped.

Lily met James's gaze, worry in her eyes. "Talia had to sneak away from her boyfriend. I'm worried about her. She's in over her head.... She's just a kid."

Stephanie's normally smooth forehead crumpled with disbelief. "She's hardly a kid. I think you should be less concerned about Talia and more concerned about your research."

Lily pushed her thin shoulders back. "Trust me, I am. But first we have to make sure Talia's okay."

"We found a rat at Talia's home," James said, sitting down next to Lily. "Maybe Talia's more involved than she claims. Didn't you say she had a lot of student debt? Maybe she thought she could sell Regen. Pay off her debt."

"She claimed Frank planted the rat in her closet," Lily said.

Stephanie shook her head, her long ponytail sweeping across her back. "We need to find her. Regen is Medlink's financial future."

"I called the chief of police. He's putting a 'be on the lookout'—or whatever it's called—

on her." He smiled at Lily, trying to reassure her. "They'll find her. We'll get to the bottom of this." A sinking feeling roiled his gut.

Lily pushed to her feet. Her hair was a mess of curls from the humidity. "I'm having a hard time getting my head around this. Talia has been nothing but a solid researcher. Now we're expected to believe she's involved with a man who stole our research and then tried to break into the clinic. Why the clinic?"

"Don't you watch the news?" Stephanie asked. "It's always the quiet ones."

"Maybe the clinic wasn't actually the target. Maybe you were," James said, the tiny hairs on the back of his neck prickling to life.

"But why hurt—" Lily's face grew deathly white "—me if he already had what he wanted?"

"To keep you from finding out," James said, his voice low and cool.

Lily pressed her palm to her forehead. James stepped a little closer, ready to react if necessary. "I'm afraid for Talia's safety if this Frank guy finds out she came to me." Lily ran a hand under her nose. "I'm afraid for her mental well-being, too. We need to find her. Help her. Straighten the rest out later."

"Talia puts absolutely everything you've worked for all these years at risk and you want to help her?" Stephanie shifted her weight and scooped up her purse, signaling she was done talking about this. "Give me a break. You're the one who's naive."

"I'll have to deal with the research aspect later," Lily said quietly. "For now, I'm worried about Talia."

"What do you think happened?" His grandfather slowly lowered himself into the chair next to his wife. Without taking his eyes from Lily, he reached over and pulled his wife's hand into his lap and patted it reassuringly.

"I think she's stressed and snapped," Lily said.

Stephanie threw her hands up. "Of course she snapped. Who cuts a hole in a chain-link fence and sneaks into her employer's home?"

Lily let out a long, slow breath, as if buying time to rein in her emotions. "You didn't see the home where she lived with her mother…." Her voice trailed off. "She's obviously had a tough life."

"Talia did have a difficult home life." James hesitated to say too much more for fear of invading Talia's privacy.

His cousin adjusted her purse strap on her shoulder. "Would you like to give her a raise and a corner office at Medlink? What kind of business are we running?"

"My first concern is finding her," Lily said. "Someone needs to go to her house. Check on

Talia's mother." James studied Lily's face. Her mask of composure slipped a little bit.

Lily tipped her head. "Thank you." She ran a hand over her hair.

"This is going to be a PR nightmare. A loose-cannon researcher." Stephanie shook her head, obviously disgusted. "This could ruin us financially."

The news his grandfather had shared earlier—of possible embezzlement at Medlink—ran through James's mind.

Pushing on his cane with a shaky hand, his grandfather stood up. "What do you think, James?"

Stephanie whipped around. "What does *he* think?" Anger rolled off her in waves. "He's going to side with his girlfriend over there." She flicked her hand at Lily.

James fisted his hands, but held his tongue.

"You are every bit your mother's daughter." His grandfather's face shook with fury. "She was as headstrong as you're being now."

"I'm not my mother's daughter." Stephanie angled her chin in such a way she reminded James of their grandmother. "I have done so much more with my life than *she* ever did."

"Stephanie," his grandmother soothed, "we're all just frazzled." His grandmother rubbed his grandfather's hand. "Don't speak poorly about your mother."

Stephanie waved a hand in dismissal. "I have to make a few phone calls. We have to hide the news from investors that the Regen files may have been stolen."

James put his hand on Lily's forearm. She stiffened under his touch. "Will you be okay staying in the carriage house or do you want me to ask Edna to prepare a room in the main house?"

"Security checked everything out?"

He nodded.

"I'd rather stay in the carriage house. I need some time alone."

James made a check of the small apartment. Lily's gaze slid toward the door, reassuring herself she had flipped the dead bolt after they'd come in. Seated on a stool at the kitchen island, she couldn't shake the horrible sense of violation. Talia had been right there.

In her apartment.

James reemerged from checking the bedroom, compassion in his eyes. He straddled the stool next to hers. "You look tired."

Resting her elbow on the counter, she played with a long strand of hair. "I am. But I doubt if I'll sleep. It'll take a while to come down off this adrenaline high. My nerves are buzzing." She ran her palm across the smooth granite. Suddenly, she bolted upright. "What about the lab? Is it secure? Security knows not to let Talia into the lab, right?"

"Absolutely. They've reset the badge readers. You'll have to go through security and get your badge reset. None of the magnetic strips on the old badges will work."

Lily slid off the stool. "I should let Sarah know. She won't be able to get into the lab, either."

James grabbed her wrist and led her back to the stool. "Security will let her know in the morning. It's fine. Sit. Relax. Take care of yourself."

She rubbed her hands up and down her arms, trying to shake the chill. "Yeah, I suppose you're right." She took a step toward the couch, then turned to James. "I don't know what scares me more. This Frank guy hurting Talia, or Talia trying to hurt herself. I've never known anyone to look so desperate. I should have stopped her." She bit her lower lip, unable to derail her erratic thinking.

James cupped her shoulder, his smooth voice washing over her. "You can't control anyone's actions but your own. Don't do this to yourself."

"I should have done something more. Talia

came to me for a reason. She wanted help." She covered her face with her hands and dropped her head until her hands hit the counter. "How come I couldn't reach her?"

"Talia is a grown woman. She's not your responsibility."

Lily lifted her head. "I feel like my world is closing in around me." She was ashamed she lacked faith.

"The police are looking for Talia. They'll find her."

"I pray they do." She searched his face but couldn't find the comfort she so badly needed.

A knock on the door startled her. James smiled and patted her hand. "It's fine. I invited Kara over."

"Why?" Exhaustion weighed heavily on her shoulders. She wasn't sure she was up for her chatty friend tonight. Kara would surely pester her for every last detail. Details she wanted to forget.

If only for tonight.

"I don't want you to be alone, and it wouldn't be appropriate for me to stay—even on the couch." A smile touched his lips. "We don't want to give Edna and Charlie anything to gossip about."

"Edna and Charlie are rooting for us." She laughed. James narrowed his gaze at her and she waggled her fingers toward the door. "Go. Answer the door." She tracked James's confident stride across the room. He opened the door a fraction, then pulled it open wide.

Kara brushed past him and rushed over to Lily. Her friend wrapped her arms around her and pulled her into a fierce embrace. "Are you okay?"

Lily smiled wanly over her shoulder at James. Stiffening, she pulled away from Kara. "I'm fine. Talia just wanted to talk." She didn't know why she was defending someone who had shaved at least ten years off her life.

"I always thought she was a tad off." Kara tossed her quilted bag on the couch.

Lily sat back on the stool and watched her friend breeze around the small apartment. "Did you ever meet her boyfriend?" Lily asked.

"No, we weren't that close. I only ate lunch with her in the cafeteria." Kara unzipped her bag, pulled out a pair of slippers, tossed them on the ground and slipped them onto her feet. "To be honest, I wondered if she was making him up because he seemed to come out of left field. Before then, she only talked about work and her plans to get her Ph.D." Kara crossed her arms and leaned against the back of the couch. "Why all the questions about her boyfriend?"

James gave Lily a nod of approval. "Her

boyfriend is the man who attacked me at the clinic and—"

"The guy who's been stalking you?" Kara's eyes grew wide. "I can't believe it. Why?"

"We're trying to figure all that out." James dug his cell phone out of his back jeans pocket. "Excuse me a minute." He turned around and answered a call.

"So are we safe here?" Kara asked.

"Yeah, the police and the head of Medlink security double-checked everything."

Kara nodded. She grabbed a bottled water from the fridge. Twisting off the cap, she rounded the couch and flopped down. "This is unbelievable. You think you know someone."

Lily sat on the arm of the couch, watching James's concerned face as he talked quietly into the phone. "How well do you really know anyone?"

James ended the call. "That was the hospital. Mrs. Benson was admitted. She's asking for me."

"Go, go." Lily got up and walked over to James. The thought of Mrs. Benson's beautiful granddaughter, Chloe, came to mind. The elderly woman had been in the clinic many times recently. "Is her granddaughter being cared for?"

"Yes. The nurse said she was staying with a neighbor." He scrubbed a hand across his face.

She wasn't the only one fighting exhaustion. "You guys okay here?"

"Yes, we're fine." She tipped her head toward Kara, who had a few DVDs in her hand. "I think my friend has a romantic-comedy marathon planned."

"Looks like you're in good hands." Leaning in close, he brushed a kiss across her cheek. "Sleep well."

Warmth spiraled around her heart. Lily met his steady gaze. "Good night."

"Hey, don't I get a kiss?" Kara held up her arm in a languid manner and let it flop over the back of the couch.

James took her hand and patted it with the other in a strictly platonic gesture. "You know I only have eyes for Lily." He turned and winked at Lily.

Lily punched him playfully on the arm. "Now go. I'm tired."

Lily ushered James to the door. He turned around in the threshold. "Make sure you turn the dead bolt. I'm going to run to the hospital and check on Mrs. Benson, then I'm coming back to the main house. I'll be staying there tonight. Call me if you need anything."

"I'll be fine," she whispered, closing the door. She turned the dead bolt; the thud of it hitting home reassured her.

"Must be nice to have money."

Lily jumped and spun around. Kara was standing right behind her. Lily pressed a hand over her racing heart. "I didn't know you were right there. Don't sneak up on me like that."

Kara held out her arms and spun around slowly, laughing. "This place is only so big. How far away can I be?" She stopped and leaned toward Lily, locking gazes. "A little jumpy, maybe?"

Lily brushed past her and sat on the couch. Leaning back, she pressed the heels of her hands into her eyes. "This is really a mess, isn't it?"

"Yes, my friend, it is." Kara sat down next to her.

Lily sat up ramrod straight. "How do you always stay composed, rational?"

"You don't have to deal with Mrs. Elinor O'Reilly day in and day out." Lifting both hands out in front of her, she pinched her fingers together. "Ohmmmm…"

"I'm not going to touch that one. I have nothing but gratitude for the O'Reillys. I wouldn't be where I am today without them."

"Me, neither." Kara giggled. "But it isn't exactly the place of my dreams. But I suppose I shouldn't complain. If Mrs. and Dr. O'Reilly take off on the cruise around the world, I may be out of a job."

"We both can fly the coop." Lily started to giggle and couldn't stop until tears rolled down her cheeks. "I might not have a choice if Talia's boyfriend stole my research." Saying the words out loud made her feel queasy.

Kara's jaw dropped. "Did he really do that?"

"That's what Talia said." The woozy feeling made her cheeks grow warm. "Talia brought him into the lab. He could have made copies of the files. No one would be the wiser. Talia was mad at me because she thought I didn't provide a strong letter of recommendation for the Ph.D. program."

"Maybe she's lying." Something dark flickered in Kara's eyes. She reached over and tapped her friend's knee. "After everything else, maybe she's a liar. Where's that faith you're always talking about?" The smile slid from Kara's face.

Lily studied her friend's face. "What's wrong?"

"I did something really awful."

Lily's mouth grew dry.

"It's about the letter of recommendation for Talia to the university."

Lily nodded, a lump forming in her throat.

"I threw it out." Kara crossed her arms, then let them drop. "She deserved it." She hiked her chin, but Lily could tell her conviction was slipping. "Talia's such a braggart. I thought she'd be insufferable if we all had to start calling her 'doctor.' And when I saw you drop the letter off in the mail room…"

Lily covered her mouth. "I can't believe you did that. You had no right."

Kara hung her head in her hands. "I know. Now look at the mess I created."

FOURTEEN

The next morning, James jogged up the stairs to Lily's second-floor apartment. He pounded on the door, the thumping competing with the pounding in his chest. He pulled his phone out of his back pocket. It was nine-fifteen in the morning. Last time he'd heard from her was shortly after he'd left last night, when Lily had called to tell him what Kara had done with Talia's letter of recommendation. He was still shaking his head over that one.

But where was Lily now? She hadn't answered her cell phone when he'd tried to call her from the main house. And Kara didn't answer her cell phone, either. Lifting his hand, he pounded again. "Come on, Lily. Answer."

He turned his back to the door and scanned the property. The sun had burned off the early-morning fog. The flowers Charlie so diligently tended lined the fence of the pool in a neat row of purples and pinks, his grandmother's favorite colors. Nothing looked out of place. He slid a finger across the screen of his cell phone and dialed her number. Again.

"Where are you?" he muttered to himself while the phone rang. A wave of apprehension coursed through him. More than once, people he loved had been taken away from him.

Without any warning.

Dread and a heavy feeling of loss constricted his chest. He forced air into his lungs. He was a grown man. He shouldn't react this way. He had taken every precaution to keep Lily safe. She was safe.

Dear Lord, please let her be safe. The prayer seemed to come as naturally as when he'd prayed as a child with his mother. The realization made him pause for the briefest of moments. He lifted his hand again and was about to knock when he heard a rustling inside.

The door handle rattled and he sucked in a breath. The door opened. Lily's tired eyes looked up at him. "What's wrong?" She pressed the heel of her hand into one eye. Pillow marks lined her cheek.

"You're home." He cupped her shoulders as if to reassure himself she was really safe and sound, standing in front of him.

"I overslept." Stepping back into the room, away from his grasp, she touched her hair self-consciously. One side was pushed up into a big lump. She had on an oversize T-shirt and cotton pajama bottoms. He had to smile. He had never seen a more beautiful sight.

He tipped his head. “May I come in?”

Lily opened the door wider. “Of course.” She held out her hand. “Don’t mind how I’m dressed.”

James brushed past her into the small apartment. “I got worried when I couldn’t get ahold of you or Kara.”

Lily sat on the stool, obviously trying to shake the sleep. “I slept like the dead.” She blinked rapidly. “I can’t think straight.” She pushed to a standing position, glanced toward the couch then flopped back down on the stool like a marionette whose strings had suddenly been plucked.

“Kara’s gone.” A pillow and a folded blanket were stacked on the arm of the couch. “Hmm…” She scratched her head. Leaning across the center island, she dragged her purse toward her. She undid the flap and dug around inside until she produced her cell phone. She glanced at the button on the edge of the phone. “Sorry. I had it on vibrate, but I don’t think I would have heard it anyway.” She scrolled through the missed calls. “Kara tried to reach me, too. I didn’t hear her leave this morning.” She narrowed her gaze. “I think she’s feeling pretty bad about what she did.”

"She should. Maybe that's why she didn't answer my call."

Lily jerked back her head. "Has something happened?"

James nodded, wishing he could spare her more bad news.

Lily's blood ran cold. James had done a good job of schooling his expression, probably to spare her, but she was tired. Tired of needing protection. Tired of hiding away in this carriage house. And tired of having this Frank Smith guy ruin her life.

"Tell me." Her intuition kicked in and sent tingles of panic slithering across her fingertips. "Something happened to Talia." Time seemed to stretch in front of her. *Please let Talia be okay.*

James closed his eyes briefly. "I'm afraid so."

Her spine went limp. She held up her hand to stop him from saying any more. She slid off the stool and moved to the couch. She pressed her hands together and tucked them between her knees. James sat on the coffee table in front of her. She met his gaze, mentally bracing herself. "Okay. Tell me."

"Talia's mother found her unresponsive in bed early this morning."

The details of the room seemed magnified in Lily's adrenaline-soaked state. She swore she could see every petal in detail in the bouquet on the center of the coffee table. "Is Talia…?" The word *dead* got stuck in her throat.

"She's alive. She's in ICU. That's all I know. The chief of police called me. He couldn't tell me any more."

"Oh, no…." Lily's gaze darted around the room, as if the answer might be in the well-appointed accessories in the apartment. "Where's Mrs. York?"

"At home. She refuses to leave the house."

Lily pushed off the couch and ran a hand through her mussed hair. "We need to see how she is." She covered her mouth and tried to tamp down her emotions. "I can't imagine how she's doing. She's probably all alone."

"I'll take you."

She froze and ran a hand down her pajama bottoms. "Give me ten minutes."

The Yorks' house—in its state of disrepair—seemed even more ominous this morning, despite the sun poking through the heavy tree branches. Lily scanned the front of the house. The front door was closed and the blinds were drawn. Mrs. York was probably in a state of shock and in no mood for visitors. But Lily wouldn't take no for an answer. No one should be alone at a time like this. As it was, the hospital told them that no one besides family would be able to visit Talia in the ICU. And due to privacy laws, they couldn't get any updated information on Talia.

"Let's go," James said, obviously sensing her hesitation.

Lily had seen the desperation in Talia's eyes. The poor girl had tried to take her own life. In her home. Her childhood bedroom. Had she hoped her mother would find her before it was too late? Had it been a cry for help that almost went unnoticed? Hadn't the police checked her home last night after Talia had shown up at the carriage house?

Why didn't you stop her? The voice in her head mocked. *She came to you. You should have stopped her.*

Lily drew in a deep breath.

James grabbed a plastic bag from the trunk and handed one to Lily. They had picked up a few fresh food items from the grocery store for Mrs. York. He slammed the back hatch and placed his hand on Lily's back, leading her up the path. She stumbled over a piece of broken concrete and quickly steadied herself. The wood steps to the porch creaked under their weight. Lily slipped her free hand into her pants pocket and held her breath. James knocked on the door and slanted her a glance, offering her a weak smile. Muffled sounds from the television could be heard through the closed door.

They waited a few minutes. No answer.

"Let me try." Lily pulled open the screen door and turned the handle on the inside door, its green paint chipping. It was unlocked. She pushed it open. The stale smell of accumulated junk assaulted her nose. Through the partially opened door, she called, "Mrs. York, it's Lily McAllister and James O'Reilly. We wanted to check on you. Make sure you're okay."

The thump-drag of Mrs. York's walker sounded down the hallway. The older woman stopped halfway to the door and ran a shaky hand under her nose. "Did you hear my Talia's in the hospital?"

"Yes. I'm sorry. I've been praying for her." Lily leaned on the doorframe. James rested his hand on her back. "That's why we stopped by. We wanted to make sure you're okay."

Mrs. York's nose flared and she shook her head. "I did my best, but she was always a weak flower. Just like her father."

James's shoulder held the screen door open. "May we come in?"

Mrs. York gave a quick nod and turned around, thumping her way back to the family room with her walker.

James nudged Lily forward. “We brought some food. May I put the things in your kitchen?”

Mrs. York lifted a shaky hand in the general direction of the kitchen. “I told you I got plenty of food.” Her tone held an air of indignation.

Despite her protests, Lily put the refrigerated items away and James stacked the other things on the counter. When they returned to the living room, they found Mrs. York in her oversize chair with threadbare arms. Lily removed some magazines from a nearby chair, her fingers brushing across something sticky. Discreetly wiping her hand on her pant leg, she lowered herself onto the chair, the springs jabbing the backs of her legs.

Leaning forward, Lily rested her elbows on her thighs. “I know you don’t need food, but there are a few things in the refrigerator and on the counter.”

Mrs. York scrunched her nose as if Lily had told her she had smeared a ripe banana across her cabinets.

“Please, tell us, what can we do for you?” Lily knew drawing the older woman’s hands into her own wouldn’t be well received.

Mrs. York looked up, her hardened eyes suddenly turned soft, watery, catching Lily off guard. “Bring my Talia back.”

Lily pressed a fisted hand to her mouth, holding back the crushing emotion of a teenage girl who had lost her mother. James brushed his fingers across Lily's shoulder. She looked up and fixed her gaze on him. The compassion in his eyes touched her soul. She was the first to look away.

Lily snapped her attention back to Mrs. York. "Would you like us to take you to the hospital?"

Mrs. York's eyes flared wide. "Oh, no, I don't want to go to the hospital.... My mother went in because she wasn't feeling good and got an infection something fierce. She died in the hospital." She reached across, grabbed a tissue and blew loudly into it. "I'm afraid my Talia's never coming home, either."

"Oh, don't say that. We have to have faith." Guilt and compassion weighed heavily on Lily. *Please, Lord, let Talia be okay.* Had Lily done everything in her power to help Talia prior to this point? Had she been too wrapped up in her own life? Her own problems?

"James and I would be happy to go with you to the hospital." Lily tried again. "It might make you feel better to see Talia."

Mrs. York's thin eyebrows twitched. All the years of being told one thing and experiencing another were etched into the lines around her flat mouth. "I already told you. I ain't going to no hospital."

The trill of James's cell phone broke the tension-filled pause. He slipped it out of his pocket and frowned at the screen. "This is important." He walked away, out of earshot.

Lily waited as long as her anxiety would allow, then met him in the front hall, careful not to trip on the stacks of newspapers cluttering the hallway. "What is it? Is it…?" She lowered her voice so Mrs. York wouldn't hear. "Is it Talia?"

"No, it's Mrs. Benson." He cupped Lily's elbow. "I have to go to the hospital. I can drop you off home first."

Unease twisted Lily's insides. "No, I can't leave Mrs. York. Not yet." She covered his hand with hers. "Go on. I can call Kara or someone for a ride in a little while. Go. Mrs. Benson needs you." The elderly woman's lonely smile and salt-and-pepper hair floated to mind.

James seemed to hesitate for a moment. "I suppose no one knows you're here. That's good. Do me a favor. Lock the doors and don't go outside until your ride is here." He pinned her with a gaze. "And if you can't catch a ride, call me. Okay? We still don't know where this Frank guy is."

"Go," she said. She got up on her tiptoes and brushed a kiss across his cheek. His scent, a mixture of soap and aftershave, reached her nose. A pleasant substitute for the stale air swirling inside the Yorks' cluttered house. "Go on. I'll be fine."

On the drive to the hospital, James caught himself reciting a prayer his mother had taught him as a child. He stopped, and then continued, the words bringing him comfort. Mrs. Benson needed his prayers. So did Talia.

And Lily.

It unnerved him to leave Lily alone at the Yorks' house. To provide a measure of peace, he called the police chief and asked him if he could have someone patrol the Yorks' street. Keep an eye on things. His friend was more than willing to oblige.

James zipped into the parking spot, jumped out of the car and jogged toward the entrance. The doors whirred open on the small country hospital, belching out cool air. Big-city folks might complain about the quaint, rural facility, but it provided a service people in poor countries could never dream of. And James's clinic bridged the gap for those who lacked insurance.

"Excuse me, sir. May I help you?"

James blinked, adjusting his eyes after coming in from the bright sunshine. A young woman sat at the main desk, watching him expectantly.

"Yes. I'm Dr. James O'Reilly. I need a pass to

see Mrs. Benson. I believe she's on the second floor, south wing."

The woman pressed a few keys on the keyboard. She studied the computer screen for a moment before glancing at him, her one eye twitching. She seemed to shake herself, before peeling off a purple visitor's pass from the roll and handing it to him. "Please stop by the nurses' station on two south before going to Mrs. Benson's room." She smiled, but it didn't reach her eyes. He didn't want to read more into her expression than he feared.

"Thank you." He slapped the sticker onto his shirt. He bypassed the elevator and entered the stairwell, the solid fire door slamming behind him. He took the stairs two at a time.

During the phone call, the nurse had said he needed to come in right away, but she hadn't been able to say any more. When the same nurse saw him jogging down the hall, she slowly stood up. The somber expression on her face made his stomach seize. Slowing his pace, he stared at her, praying for a smile. A nod of reassurance. Anything. Something.

Nothing.

"I'm sorry, Dr. O'Reilly. Mrs. Benson died fifteen minutes ago. I had hoped she'd hang on long enough for you to get here. I know how much she meant to you."

James plastered on a polite smile and pointed toward the room where Mrs. Benson had chatted with him last night. When she had told him of her wishes. Her hopes for her granddaughter's future. "Is she still…?"

"Yes."

James walked toward the hospital room. Time slowed to a crawl. His shoes creaked against the linoleum floor as he entered the room. A privacy curtain shielded the bed. Gulping around a knot of emotion, he slid the curtain back just enough to slip through. He had seen much death in his life, but he had never witnessed one so peaceful. Something shifted in his heart. The nurse had placed Mrs. Benson's hands one on top of the other. If he hadn't run into the nurse, he might have suspected Mrs. Benson had dozed off into a restful sleep.

He covered her cool hand with his and lowered himself into the vinyl chair. He wondered if Mrs. Benson had died while he was reciting the prayer on the drive over. The prayer his mother had taught him. A measure of peace settled in his heart. *Dear Lord, let her rest in peace.*

The curtain hooks rattled in their tracks. The nurse stood in the opening, compassion radiating from every gesture. "Do you need more time, Dr. O'Reilly? The funeral home is here to take care of Mrs. Benson."

James slowly stood. "Tell them I'll be right out." The nurse turned to walk away and he called to her. "Do you know where her granddaughter is?"

"I was just about to call social services. She'll need to be picked up from the neighbor's." The nurse's lower lip trembled. "It's so sad. First that child lost her mother—now her grandmother."

James tugged on his ear. "Do you have the number of the contact at social services? I'll call." Mrs. Benson had been very specific in her final wishes. Guilt niggled at him. He wished he had been more up front with his elderly patient.

The nurse's eyes opened a fraction wider. "Oh, okay. If you're sure, Dr. O'Reilly?"

"Yes, I'm sure." He followed the nurse to her desk, where she wrote down the information.

He pointed to the phone on her cluttered desk. "May I use this?" The nurse nodded. He picked up the receiver and dialed. He shifted the phone to his other hand and ran his palm down his pant leg.

Lily heated up soup and fixed a salad for Mrs. York from the items they had purchased at the grocery store. She found a TV tray and set it in the family room in front of Mrs. York's chair. Lily had to do a lot of rearranging to clear a spot for the tray. She had no idea how someone could live like this. Lily would have to see about getting Mrs. York assistance to clean her home, especially if Talia didn't… No, she couldn't think that way. Once Talia was better, she'd work with both of them to get this house in order. She'd get Mrs. York the help to keep it clean.

Mrs. York seemed to harrumph when Lily placed the food in front of her, but she ate it with no complaint. When Mrs. York was done, she leaned back in her chair and crossed her arms over her belly. "I don't know why you're fussing over me."

"I want to make sure you're okay." Lily knew what it was like to be totally alone after losing someone close. She didn't know what she would have done if the O'Reillys—and Edna—hadn't been so generous with her after her mother died. Her sister, Bethany, had been traveling the country with a boyfriend and couldn't be bothered with her little sister.

Not a day went by that Lily didn't thank God for her blessings. Where would she be today if the O'Reillys hadn't taken her in and paid for her education?

"Earth to Lily." Mrs. York's gruff voice broke through her trance.

"Yes? Can I get you anything else?" Lily stood in front of the TV tray, preparing to take it away.

Mrs. York shooed her with the TV remote.

Lily stepped aside, not realizing she had been blocking the screen. The older woman pointed the remote at the television, turning the volume up on a late-afternoon talk show. Without looking at Lily, she said, "Don't let me keep you."

Knowing the woman was hurting, scared, lonely, Lily ignored her biting comments. Lily decided she couldn't leave until she at least cleaned up the dirty dishes, not that it would make a dent in the mess in this small ranch. But she had to do something. *Feel* as if she was doing something. And it would be wrong to leave Mrs. York alone.

She carried the dishes into the kitchen and set them on the counter. An unexpected feeling of hope bubbled up. Maybe James would call from the hospital with good news. Bracing her arms on the kitchen sink, she said another prayer for Mrs. Benson, Talia…and for Mrs. York. *May Talia recover and may both mother and daughter find peace.*

Lily busied herself washing dishes and tidying the countertops. She found a large garbage bag under the sink and tossed most everything out. She might have been a little forward, but something had to be done. She tied off the bag and set it by the back door.

She pulled back the lacy curtain covering the window on the door and remembered her promise to James not to go outside unless she had a ride waiting. The clutter in the yard provided ample opportunity for someone to hide. To watch the house. To stalk her. A chill surged down her spine, shattering her fleeting hope.

A part of her was surprised—disappointed, almost—James hadn't checked in with her. He had left hours ago. She closed her eyes, and Mrs. Benson's beautiful granddaughter came to mind. The little girl was a handful, but what a blessing the grandmother had come into Chloe's life when her mother was unable to care for her.

Lily pressed her steepled fingers to her lips, remembering Chloe's sweet smile. Lily was grateful for her faith. It kept her grounded during times like these. Without her faith, she would have fallen into a dark hole with no hope.

A soft moaning sounded from the family room. Lily tossed down the dish towel and ran to the family room, stumbling over a stack of magazines near the doorway. She flattened her hand against the wall to steady herself and knocked a photo of a young family of three off-kilter, no doubt the York family at a happier time. Talia, wearing pigtails, a red dress and a lopsided grin, couldn't have been more than five in the photo.

Lily reached Mrs. York, who was down on the floor on her hands and knees, whimpering. The TV tray was upended next to her.

Lily knelt and tried to assess the situation. "What happened?"

"Oh, it hurts."

Lily grabbed her forearm. "Can you stand?"

"Oh, I don't know."

Lily touched the older woman's shoulder. "Maybe I should call an ambulance."

Mrs. York shook her head vehemently. "Oh, no. I don't want anyone coming into my house. They'll come in here—" she gulped "—and tell me I can't live here." She lifted her head and pleaded with her eyes. "Help me into my chair."

"We have to be careful. You shouldn't move. What's hurt?"

"Please help me into my chair." Mrs. York's tone grew desperate.

Against her better judgment, Lily grabbed Mrs. York's forearm and helped her into the chair. The older woman grimaced, closing her eyes against the pain. "That stupid tray was in my way. I caught my foot on it."

Lily felt a certain amount of indignity in it all. Stacks of newspapers, magazines and discarded items littered the house, but the TV tray Lily had set up was what Mrs. York had tripped on. Lily's gaze drifted down the length of her. She stifled a groan when she noticed Mrs. York's left foot turned at an awkward angle.

"We should go to the hospital and have your leg checked out."

"Oh, no." A tear slipped down the older woman's cheek. It was her first real show of emotion.

"Can I look at it?" Lily gently touched her pant leg.

"No, no, no…."

The stale air weighed heavily on Lily's lungs. A trickle of sweat dripped between her shoulder blades. "Would you let me take you to the clinic? I can call James. Have him meet us there." Maybe once he checked her out, he could convince her to get the care she needed at the hospital.

Mrs. York ran her hands up and down the worn arms of her chair and then nodded.

Lily pulled out her cell phone. With Mrs. York quietly weeping in the background, she dialed James's number. Frustration and panic wound like twin ribbons around her chest when he didn't answer his phone. *Where are you, James?*

She pressed End and called the O'Reillys' home. Stephanie answered the phone, but she hadn't seen James. Once Lily explained her predicament, Stephanie promised to use her connections to reach James at the hospital. She encouraged Lily to take Mrs. York to the clinic, and she assured her she'd find James and send him right over.

* * *

Once they reached the clinic, Lily paid the cabdriver, then got out and walked around to open the door for Mrs. York. Nancy, the nurse practitioner on duty at the clinic, met her with a wheelchair. Mrs. York moaned as the two women jockeyed her from the cab into the wheelchair.

The nurse's gaze slid down to Mrs. York's swollen ankle. "We can't do X-rays here."

Lily pressed a finger to her lips and lowered her voice. "Let's see what we can do for her at the clinic. For now." Nancy slipped her hands into the pockets of her scrubs and gestured with her elbow toward the entrance ramp. Lily smiled her thanks and pushed Mrs. York through the front doors.

"I'll get her something for the pain." Nancy strode toward the back of the house, where they kept the medications. Her movements held the urgency of a nurse used to handling a million tasks at once.

Lily sat next to Mrs. York in the empty lobby. The clinic had closed five minutes ago and Nancy had stayed to open the door for them. "Are you doing okay, Mrs. York?"

The older woman gave her an annoyed expression that had become all too familiar. No wonder Talia was always so down on herself. "I'd feel better if I were at home watching my programs." She narrowed an accusatory gaze at Lily. "If you hadn't put that TV tray right where I'd trip on it."

Lily bit back her frustration and checked the clock on the wall. *Where is James?* Surely, Stephanie had tracked him down by now.

Nancy appeared with two small cups. One with medication and another with water. "Do you have any allergies, Mrs. York?"

Mrs. York shook her head. "No, I'm healthy as a horse."

The nurse tipped her head as if she had heard that a million times before. "Well, here you go, then." The older woman took them without complaint.

Nancy turned to Lily. "I have a babysitter...."

Lily forced a smile. She didn't relish the idea of being left alone at the clinic, but she couldn't expect Nancy to stay any later. The nurse had already put in a long day. "Go on. James should be here soon." *Please let James arrive soon.*

Lily saw Nancy out the front door and locked it behind her. She turned on the TV in the waiting room and flipped the channels until Mrs. York seemed content.

A loud rapping at the back door made Lily jump. Her heart lurched and her gaze instinctively went to the clock mounted on the wall. Patients came to the front door. Not the back.

Besides, the clinic was closed.

An image of Frank Smith's warped features filtered into her brain. Clasping her cell phone in hand, she crept along the long corridor. She was unable to shake the foreboding clutching at her throat. She slipped into the last examining room on the right and peered out the window. She let out a long rush of breath. Outside the back door, Stephanie paced, her hand poised to knock again.

Lily scrambled down the stairs and undid the bolt on the back door. "Stephanie, I wasn't expecting you."

"I wanted to tell you I couldn't get ahold of James." A crease lined her smooth forehead. "I can't imagine where he is. I figured you'd be worried." The intensity of Stephanie's gaze bored through her. "And I knew James wouldn't want you here by yourself. It's just you and Mrs. York, right?"

"Mrs. York is in the waiting room." Lily slowed by the nurses' station and rested her elbow on the high counter. "I was hoping James could convince Mrs. York to go to the hospital. I'm not having any luck." An unlikely idea slammed into her, but at this point she was desperate to try anything. "Maybe you can help me convince her."

A slow smile crept across Stephanie's perfectly lined red lips. "Why would she listen to me?"

Lily threw up her hands. "I'm at a loss. She absolutely needs to get her ankle looked at. I'm afraid it's broken."

Stephanie peeked around the corner, but stayed out of sight of Mrs. York. "I don't think she'll listen to me." She adjusted the strap of her purse on her shoulder and smoothed her hand across the leather.

A hint of cold, icy fear pumped through Lily's veins. An irrational spurt of emotion. "Did you lock the back door?"

Seemingly ignoring the question, Stephanie reached into her purse and pulled out her phone. She looked at the display for a quick second before saying, "Let me try to reach James one last time. If we can't, we transport the old—" she locked eyes with Lily, seeming to catch herself "—Mrs. York to the hospital."

A sliver of light seeped in along the frame of the back door. Lily held her breath, willing James's handsome face to appear. A shadow filled the doorway. Instinctively, Lily reached out and grabbed Stephanie's forearm, frozen with indecision.

"Hello," Lily called down the hallway. "I'm sorry. We're closed." A small part of her was holding out hope it was James. But his size was all wrong.

Too short. Too wide. Too…

The man stalked closer, lifting his head, revealing the face that had haunted her nightmares under that worn Buffalo Bills baseball cap.

Lily tugged on Stephanie's arm, quickly calculating her limited options. The ding-ding-ding of a game show on TV trickled into her subconscious. *Mrs. York.* They'd never be able to escape with a woman in a wheelchair.

The man stopped, an ugly snarl skewing the corners of his thin lips. Lily adjusted her stance. Stephanie spun around to square off with the intruder, a stiff smile plastered on her red lips. "It's about time you got here."

FIFTEEN

James approached the front door of the third apartment on the left and knocked. A cacophony of muffled noises sounded from inside the brick building. He lifted his hand to knock again when something at the window caught his eye. The thick curtain parted, revealing two little faces from their noses up, their curious eyes squarely on him. He waved and the curtain fell back. Little feet thumped across the floor. The door handle turned back and forth, as if the child didn't know how to open it. Finally, the door creaked open and a little boy around five peered out with big brown eyes.

James crouched down. "Is your mommy home?" Behind the boy, Chloe, Mrs. Benson's granddaughter, hung back, watching him with equal interest. James gave her his best *everything-is-going-to-be-okay* smile, but little Chloe had yet to learn her grandmother wasn't coming back. Ever. Maybe she'd never fully understand.

James drew in a deep breath.

"JJ, you're not supposed to answer the door." Somewhere deeper in the house, a woman scolded the young child. Her smart footsteps sounded on the floor. Wiping her hands on a dish towel, she eyed James up and down. "I'm sorry. We're not interested." She slung the towel over her shoulder and planted the palm of her hand on the door, ready to slam it in his face.

James stepped forward, blocking the door. The woman glared at him. Not wanting to scare her, James retreated a step and held up his palms. "I'm Dr. James O'Reilly. Are you Molly Hopkins?"

The young woman nodded. "Yes…?" Her answer came out more as a question. "Is something wrong?"

James's gaze dropped to the two children staring up at him from the doorway. She waved the dish towel, shooing away the kids. "Go on now. Go and check on your big sister. The adults need to talk here. Mind your manners." Her eyes remained fixed on James's face. The annoyance lining her eyes softened and morphed into something more akin to fear, worry.

Molly held on to the edge of the door, as if she needed something to prop her up. "Is it Mrs. Benson?"

James reached out to touch her arm to offer

her comfort, but he dropped his hand when he noticed her flinch. "Mrs. Benson passed away this afternoon. I'm sorry."

A tear glistened in the corner of Molly's eye and she sucked in her lower lip between her teeth. Slowly, she blinked, seemingly in a mighty effort to control her emotions. "Oh, dear. That sweet, sweet woman." Her shoulders sagged and her knuckles grew white on the edge of the door.

"May I come in?" James asked. "I think you'd be more comfortable if you sat down." She searched his face, a decision flickering behind her eyes. A person didn't let strangers into their home. "I'm here about Chloe," he added. "The social worker is on her way."

Molly stepped away from the door and sat on the couch under the window. She repeatedly threaded the dish towel through her hands.

"May I get you some water?"

"Yes, thank you." Molly finally found her voice.

James strode to the kitchen in the back of the small, tidy and cramped apartment. He filled a glass with water and brought it to her. She took a long sip and smiled up at him. "Thank you."

He sat on the couch next to her. Her eyes moved toward a short hallway off the family room. "What's going to happen to little Chloe? She has no one." Molly ran the back of her hand over her mouth. "And Lord knows I can't take her. I can barely feed the two mouths I have."

"Mrs. Johnston from social services is going to meet me here."

"Poor child," Molly whispered. "Poor, poor child."

Just then little Chloe ran into the room with JJ two steps behind. Chloe gave James a bright smile, an unexpected ray of sunshine on an otherwise dreary day. She boosted herself up onto the corner of the couch next to James. She grabbed a pink fleece blanket draped over the arm of the couch and rubbed it against the side of her nose. She looked up at him with big brown eyes. "Hi, Dr. James."

Something in his chest expanded. "Hi, Chloe." She had remembered him. "Is that your blankie?"

She bowed her head shyly and snuggled into the blanket.

A quiet knock sounded on the door and James answered it.

"Hello, I'm Mrs. Johnston from social services." The woman was dressed in a crisp suit, perhaps the kind of clothes one wore when they took a little girl away from the only home she'd ever known.

Molly swiped at a tear. "What's wrong, Momma?" JJ asked.

Molly scooped JJ into an embrace. He settled

contentedly on her lap. "Momma's just tired." She met James's gaze and gave him a slight nod.

James reached for Chloe's hand. She took it without hesitation. Her tiny hand in his made his heart melt. It blasted away the remaining protective wall shielding him from hurt, from healing, from having close relationships.

If you never let anyone in, you never get to experience true joy. Love. Another beautiful face came to mind. As soon as he settled things here, he'd have to find Lily. Have a frank discussion. See if she was open to a future with him.

James crouched in front of Chloe. "There's someone I'd like you to meet." He glanced at the social worker's face, her expression reflecting just the right mix of compassion and professionalism. "This is Mrs. Johnston."

The young social worker held out her hand and smiled. Chloe buried her face in James's leg. He reached down and smoothed his hand over her head. "It's okay." Tears burned the back of his nose. Mrs. Benson had loved this child dearly and had asked him to see that she was well cared for.

"Where is she going to go?" Molly asked, alarm in her voice.

Mrs. Johnston's gaze locked with his. "Into a foster home. For now," she seemed to add as an afterthought.

Molly pushed to her feet. "Is there any way she can stay here? For a few more days?" Her gaze darted around the cramped room. "I could manage for a few more days...please."

Mrs. Johnston seemed to consider it a moment.

"Mrs. Benson always spoke highly of Molly." James bent down and picked up Chloe, and Mrs. Johnston nodded slightly. He hooked a finger under Chloe's little chin. "Would you like to hang out with JJ?"

Chloe hugged her blankie tighter. "Want Gammy."

James closed his eyes briefly, praying for wisdom. "I know." He gave her a quick hug and put her down. "You stay here and play with JJ. I'll come back and see you soon."

JJ took Chloe's hand, the protective older brother. "Let's play with my building blocks."

Chloe looked up at James, smiled, and then the two children ran off together.

"Thank you, Molly." James breathed a sigh of relief. "I'll bring some groceries in the morning."

The social worker nodded. "You realize this is only a temporary situation."

"I know. I have some things to figure out." James ran his hand across the back of his neck. He had yet to break the news to Chloe about her grandmother's passing.

"You have my number." The social worker waved, then turned, exited the apartment and walked down the sidewalk. He watched her climb into a small sedan and drive away. He pulled out his cell phone. He had put the phone on silent mode when he had entered the hospital. Then his day had spiraled out of control after he'd learned of Mrs. Benson's death. He frowned at the missed-call indicator. He muttered under his breath when he realized every call but one had been from Lily.

"What's going on back there?" Mrs. York hollered, concern edging her brash tone. "I'm awfully tired. I'd like to go home. I can hardly keep my eyes open. What did that nurse give me?"

"Tell her everything is okay," Stephanie whispered, enunciating each word. When Lily balked, the other woman reached out and clutched her wrist. "Tell her."

"Give me a minute, Mrs. York. I'll be right there." The fine hairs on the back of Lily's neck prickled, yet her voice sounded deceptively calm.

"What's going on?" Lily yanked her wrist free of Stephanie's death grip. "I don't know what you want—" her nostrils flared "—and I don't know what that smug jerk wants, but I'm leaving." The walls of the narrow hallway bulged and flexed in her peripheral vision. She spun around, and this time Frank grabbed her forearm and forced her down onto a stool.

"Yeah, Steph, why don't you tell the lady *doctor* why *you're* here?" Frank rested his elbow on the counter, his hoodie jacket pulling away from his waist, revealing a gun. "Don't trust me to do the job?"

Lily gasped, then quickly covered her mouth so as not to frighten Mrs. York, who was agitated with the wait, but oblivious to her plight.

Stephanie's jaw tensed. "Should I trust you to do the job?" A chill settled in the stagnant air. The thug snarled, more annoyed than offended.

Stephanie tipped her head, her long blond ponytail dragging across her shoulder. "You always seem to be in the wrong place at the wrong time recently, don't you, Lily?"

"I don't understand...." Lily stiffened her shoulders, trying to read the woman's cold, dead eyes.

Stephanie tapped her lips with a long red nail. "It's quite the change for you, isn't it? You always seemed to land on your feet. Someone always sweeps in and saves you." She stared off into the middle distance, as if some memory was playing in her mind's eye.

"Stephanie—" Lily tried to keep her voice even "—what are you talking about?"

"My grandparents treat you like another

grandchild." Stephanie's attention snapped back and landed squarely on Lily, her eyes burning through her like lasers. "If you haven't noticed, you *aren't* their granddaughter. *I'm* their granddaughter."

"Your grandparents are generous to a lot of people. Not just me." Lily tried rationalizing with an irrational person.

Stephanie rolled her eyes. "I'm over it. I got bigger problems now."

Frank stood and tugged down on his cap. "You ladies done chatting? I've got places to be."

Stephanie stroked the leather of her large designer bag. She opened her purse, reached inside and pulled out a gun. Icy fear shot through Lily's veins. Instinctively, she took a step back.

"Don't go anywhere. You won't get far. Not with the old bag out in the waiting area. And I know you won't leave her."

Stephanie slowly pivoted, pointed the gun at Frank and pulled the trigger. Frank's eyes widened and his features crumpled as if the one person he trusted had just put a bullet in his chest. He pressed his hand to his chest, removed it and squinted at his bloody fingers. A burst of red exploded on his gray T-shirt under his open jacket.

"Why?" His knees buckled under him. His jaw crashed against the counter with a horrendous crack. His lifeless body crumpled onto the floor behind the nurses' station.

Lily bit back a sob. Her legs wobbled under her. She wanted to run, escape, but she couldn't leave Mrs. York. In the fuzzy periphery of her consciousness she heard Mrs. York hollering to them. No doubt wondering what was going on.

Stephanie lifted the gun to Lily's chest. "Take one step and I kill you and the old bag."

White dots floated in Lily's line of vision. She watched as if outside herself. Stephanie grabbed a tissue, then leaned over and pulled a gun from Frank's waistband. She stood up quickly. "See, I stopped him. Just in time. Self-defense."

Taking a chance, Lily scooped up the receiver on the phone. "We need to call the police." She pointed at Frank, a red puddle forming under his body. "This is the same man who had tried to get into the clinic before." A million scenarios scraped across her aching brain. None of the puzzle pieces snapped into place.

Stephanie pressed her palm to her forehead; a trace of something Lily couldn't name flashed in her eyes. Then Stephanie's attention seemed to snap into focus. She shook her head. "Nothing's ever easy, is it?" Stephanie fisted her hand. "I only wanted what was rightfully mine." Her lips thinned into a straight line. "My mother had everything growing up. *Everything.* But she threw it all away. Hung around with the wrong people. Got herself disowned." She pounded her fist on the desk. "I had to work my whole life to get myself back into my grandparents' good graces."

"Your grandparents love you." Lily pressed together her trembling lips.

Stephanie narrowed her gaze. "As soon as James returned to Orchard Gardens, good old Declan wanted him to run Medlink." She gritted her pristine white teeth. "I've been working like a dog for Declan. *I* was supposed to run Medlink."

Lily couldn't gather enough saliva to swallow. "You know James doesn't want to run Medlink. He wants to practice medicine. You already know that." Lily scrambled to talk Stephanie off the proverbial ledge. "You'll run Medlink. Just like you always wanted to."

Stephanie scoffed. "Seriously? You really do live in la-la land." She lifted the gun. She had traded her tissue for a black leather driving glove that coordinated with her ensemble. "The only way I'm going to maintain my current lifestyle is to kill you." She raised her eyebrows. "And James."

James parked in front of the clinic on the street and stared up at the neat Victorian home. Every time he came to this place, his loyalties were torn between reenlisting and staying here and practicing medicine. Part of his indecisiveness stemmed from knowing that as long as he lived in Orchard Gardens, his grandparents would be in his ear about returning full-time to Medlink.

But now he had something else to consider. Little Chloe.

And Lily.

He rolled his shoulders, trying to ease the knot between his shoulder blades. He climbed out of the car, strode up the path and pulled on the glass door. Locked. He tented his hand and pressed it against the glass. From here, he couldn't see past the small foyer into the waiting room, but he assumed Lily and Mrs. York were still waiting for him. Nancy had called him on her way out and left a message to let him know she had closed the clinic, but Lily and an older woman were waiting for him there.

James unlocked the door and stepped inside the small foyer. The air was thick with antiseptic and something else he couldn't quite put his finger on. The stillness put him on high alert. In the waiting room, he found Mrs. York in a wheelchair, her head lolling forward at an awkward angle. "Hello!" he called, glancing around the clinic. Deep shadows stretched into the corners of the space. He touched Mrs. York's neck. Her pulse was steady.

"Hello." Stephanie appeared in the archway dressed in her regular non-work-hours uniform: black yoga pants and a black T-shirt.

James cocked his head. "Is…Lily here?"

Stephanie stepped back. Lily was sitting on the stool, a terrified look in her eyes.

"What's going on?" The fine hairs on the back of James's neck stood on edge. The coppery scent of blood filled the air. He swept his gaze over Lily from head to toe. Physically she appeared okay. *Where is that smell coming from?*

"What is going on?" he repeated.

Stephanie pulled a gloved hand out from behind her back and pointed a gun at him. Instinctively, he lifted his hands. Years of army training kicked in. But could he use deadly force against his cousin?

Stephanie took a quick step back and pressed the barrel of the gun to Lily's head. Lily closed her eyes briefly, her chest rising and falling. A tear ran down her cheek.

"Don't try anything," his cousin said.

"What in the world is going on?" Rage shook his voice.

"Why didn't you tell me you had no interest in running Medlink?" If Stephanie hadn't been holding a gun to Lily's head, he might have thought he detected concern—contrition, almost.

James flinched. "What do you mean? I told

you and Grandfather I wanted to reenlist a few days ago."

"You would have saved me a lot of trouble if you had only told me sooner. *Much sooner.* Before I made all these plans. Plans I couldn't undo. You knew how much I wanted to run Medlink." Her tone reminded him of how she used to beg their grandparents for gifts on the few times she visited as a child. "I really want the doll with the pretty blond hair."

"This is all about you wanting to be the boss?" James asked, a muscle working in his jaw.

Stephanie slid her hand under Lily's chin. "It's a shame, really. If you had only been honest, this all never had to happen." She gestured to James with her chin. "I had paid Frank to come to the clinic to kill *you.* To *kill you.* Then I would have been the logical choice for CEO of Medlink. And then this one—" she patted Lily's cheek roughly "—had to take a trip to the Dumpster. Get in the way."

A jolt shot down his spine. He fisted his hand as he locked gazes with Lily. He tried to project with his eyes that everything would be okay. *Dear God, let everything be okay.* "Why are you doing this now? If I reenlisted, the position would still be yours."

"Everything is black-and-white with you, isn't it? My friend here—" Stephanie's nose flared in disgust as if she couldn't believe her own stupidity "—got greedy."

James followed his cousin's lowered gaze and saw for the first time the man on the floor behind the nurses' station. His cold eyes stared into nothingness. "What happened?"

Stephanie dug her fingers into her scalp, then dropped her arm. She gestured with her gun at the man on the floor. "I hired this idiot to kill you."

A ringing started in James's ears. "What are you talking about?"

"With you out of the way, I'd get to run Medlink. But this idiot couldn't even do that right. On his way to stage a break-in at the clinic, he runs into Lily. Once he recognized her photo in the local paper, he realized *she* was the researcher I had stupidly told him about. He knew how valuable her research was to Medlink's future. To my future. So he blackmailed me."

Lily leaned heavily on the counter and spoke for the first time. "Frank told me he could get me whenever he wanted. Now it makes sense. He wanted Stephanie to know he could hurt me if he wanted to. That's why you were so eager to have me leave town. If he couldn't get to me, he couldn't blackmail you."

"Yes. But you wouldn't listen. You had to stay

in town." Stephanie swiped her free hand across her forehead. "You just couldn't listen."

James knew he had to keep her talking. "How did Talia get mixed up in all this?"

Stephanie narrowed her eyes, and she looked as if she wanted to hit someone. "Frank was using her. When I hired him, I told him about Lily's research. How valuable it was. He took it upon himself to hang out at the social spots around Medlink, and he eventually struck up a relationship with Talia. Frank was going to find a way to extort money out of me one way or another. He used Talia to gain access to your research. And I ended up playing right into it.

"That Talia's such a needy girl. I can't stand needy people. If I could have twisted things around, I would have made her look guilty. But she went and killed herself. And I knew this jerk wasn't going to go away."

James kept his mouth shut that Talia's suicide had been unsuccessful.

"So this has nothing to do with gang activity?" James asked.

Stephanie made a *get-real* sound. "No. That was Frank being clever. Trying to distract the police with some stupid theory that gangs were involved."

"Stephanie, you've got to stop this craziness. Please." James took a step toward her.

"You can't tell me what to do." She lifted the gun and pointed it at his chest. He froze.

"I did us all a favor. Now Frank can't try to sell your research." Stephanie's mask of indifference and her flippant tone made Lily's blood run cold. "Now that Regen is moving into clinical trials, I'm confident it will be a success, even if Lily here is not around to see it through."

"Stephanie—" James warned, a muscle ticking in his jaw "—it stops here."

Stephanie closed her eyes briefly, drawing in a deep breath. Tired. Resigned, almost. Her hand dropped from Lily's neck. James sprang off the balls of his feet and slammed Stephanie into the counter. She hit it with an *oomph.* The gun tumbled to the ground. Lily bolted from the stool and picked up the gun, holding it away from her body as if she had a rat by the tail.

James yanked Stephanie to her feet and wrenched her arm behind her back. She grunted. He glanced over his shoulder at Lily. "Lock the gun in the top of the desk and call the police."

Lily nodded, her eyes wide with shock.

"Sit on the ground, Stephanie."

His cousin slid down the wall and covered her face. James pressed his fingers to the man's throat. No pulse. James averted his gaze from all the blood, a violent image from his army days clawing at his memory.

Pivoting, he crouched next to Stephanie. "You didn't go to all this trouble because you were mad Grandfather had picked me over you to run Medlink." He angled his face to get a read on hers.

Stephanie lowered her hands and hugged her knees to her chest. She released a shuddering breath. "I stole money from Medlink." Resting an elbow on her knee, she braced her forehead in her hand. "Grandfather wasn't as involved as he used to be. No one was paying attention. I knew once you came back, you'd notice the discrepancies in the accounting." She pounded her forehead with the heel of her hand. "I am so stupid."

"Our grandparents gave you everything."

Stephanie lifted her tearstained face. "I needed the money. I lost a lot of money gam bling. I had some really bad guys after me. I had to pay them back." Her entire body shuddered. "That's how I met Frank. We became friends at the casino tables."

"So you tried to have me killed to hide the fact you were embezzling money?" He sat on a stool, his knees growing weak. His cousin. His own flesh and blood.

"I couldn't go to prison." She lifted her palms. "I couldn't lose everything I had worked so hard to get." Her flattened mouth puckered at the edges. "Lily wasn't supposed to be at the clinic that day Frank came."

"Is that supposed to make me feel better?" Rage bubbled under the surface. "So you decided you'd come here today, kill me and Lily and then blame it all on Frank."

"Yep." Cockiness returned to her expression. Lightness in her eyes. "I was going to come in and kill him in self-defense. Tie up all the loose ends."

James scratched his head. "I understand your motive to kill Frank, even me, but why Lily?"

"I thought I needed her alive for Regen, but once I learned her research was moving into clinical trials, I knew her value had plummeted. Another researcher could pick up where she had left off to find a cure, right? But for now, the treatment she had found would make Medlink rich. Maybe richer than finding a cure, thus ending the need for a treatment."

"You're evil, you know that?" James stood and her empty gaze followed him. She was huddled on the floor, a stressed-out mess. "You had everything...." Disbelief swirled in his head.

"I'll never have what you have, James." Stephanie's head dropped into her hands. "As long as you and Lily were around, our grandparents wouldn't care about me. They never really had."

"That's where you're wrong." James dragged

a hand through his hair. "Want to hear the ultimate irony, Stephanie?"

She glanced up at him with a question in her eyes.

"The other night, Grandfather told me the board of directors had audited the books. They had found some discrepancies." James shook his head. "You killed a man for nothing. You were never going to get away with embezzling money."

Stephanie slammed her head back against the wall. "Stupid, stupid, stupid."

"James?" Lily's voice snapped him out of his nightmare. "The police are here." She tipped her head toward the waiting room, where an EMT was checking on Mrs. York.

An officer strode in and arrested Stephanie. EMTs tended to Frank, but any sense of urgency seemed lost. The man was dead. As the chief led Stephanie out, he called over his shoulder, "I'll be back in to take your statements."

Lily came in from the waiting room. "Mrs. York's going to the hospital in an ambulance. She's groggy from the pain medication Nancy gave her, and she needs her leg x-rayed." Her teeth chattered.

James reached out and took her hand, pulling her into a fierce embrace. He smoothed his hand down her hair and back, and a quick shudder racked her body.

"Thank God you got here when you did," she whispered into his chest.

James tilted his head back and looked into Lily's glistening eyes. A small smile lit her face. He touched his lips to hers and thanked God.

EPILOGUE

Nine months later...

"There you are."

Lily spun around, a slow smile spreading across her face at the sight of James strolling around the side of her cottage out in the country. He had on jeans and a T-shirt on one of the first spring days warm enough to forgo a jacket. The bushes at the back of her cottage had started to sprout new buds. It was her favorite time of year.

New beginnings.

Lily inhaled deeply, smelling the damp soil, the pine needles, the fresh new scent of spring. "There *you* are. We've been waiting for you!" Lily said.

She turned around and grabbed the rope of the tire swing hanging from a huge maple tree. "Now, make sure you're holding on tight. Okay?"

Chloe tipped her head back, her braids spilling

down her back. She squealed in delight. "Higher, Momma Lily, higher," she said in the adorable way only a three-year-old could say.

"Not too high." She'd never grow tired of the way the precious child called her Momma Lily.

James came up behind Lily and slipped his arm around her waist. She lifted his hand and kissed it, the sun glinting off the gold on his ring finger. "How are you, Mrs. O'Reilly?"

She nudged him gently with her elbow. "That's Dr. McAllister-O'Reilly."

James nuzzled her neck. "It has a nice ring to it." One she was still getting used to. They had gotten married last month after a whirlwind courtship, romance and legal proceedings, which made them an instant family.

James caught the tire swing and kissed his daughter. Their daughter. Happy tears blurred Lily's vision.

"How's my peanut?" James asked, pulling the tire swing close. Chloe reached out, wrapped her arms around his neck and held on like a little koala until he dragged her off the swing.

"Momma Lily says we're gonna eat hot dogs and have a picnic."

"Is that what you want?"

Her brown eyes opened wide. "Hot dog with ketchup."

Chloe wiggled and James put her down. She

ran after the soccer ball and kicked it around the yard.

Lily tucked a strand of hair behind her ear. "Talia called me this morning." James's eyebrows drew together. "She's doing well. She's seeing a therapist." Lily shook her head. "It's so sad that she had such low self-esteem she allowed Frank Smith to manipulate her to the point she felt her only out was to try to take her life. I told her I'd help her any way I can." Lily scratched her forearm. "I think she's going to take some time to heal before making plans."

"Do you ever wonder if Talia would have gotten caught up in this if Kara hadn't sabotaged her chances of getting into the Ph.D. program?"

"I have. I don't know what Kara was thinking." She swatted at a dirt mark on her shorts where Chloe's sneaker had touched. "Maybe Kara was jealous of Talia's academic success. Regardless, she apologized to Talia and decided to leave town for a while. I think she's taking a few classes at a local college. I think Talia forgave her. Now Kara will have to forgive herself."

"Is Talia going to enroll in the Ph.D. program this fall?" James tugged at his collar. The spring sun was surprisingly warm.

"Talia needs time to heal."

"How's Mrs. York? Has she been able to keep the house clean?" James and Lily had hired professionals to work with the elderly woman to get the junk cleaned out of her house.

"Talia says she has." Lily curled her bare toes into the green grass. "I hadn't heard Talia sound as hopeful as she did today. She also mentioned they were going to church. I think things will come together for them."

James kissed her forehead. "You're a good person, you know that?"

Lily laughed. "I hope so. You married me." She spun her rings around her finger. He had given her the diamond ring his father had given his mother on their engagement.

"I wish my cousin had as bright a future." A dark cloud passed behind James's eyes.

Lily reached out and ran her thumb across the smooth flesh of the back of his hand. "I'm sorry. I know your grandparents were estranged from Stephanie's mother, but I really thought Stephanie felt welcomed. Part of the family."

James released a breath, as if he were cleansing himself of any dark thoughts. "It was her gambling habit that led her down this path. She owed money to some bad people. She figured stealing from Medlink was an easy way to pay them back." He covered her hand with his and squeezed. "But it kept snowballing, especially once Frank Smith started blackmailing her. It's a shame, really. My grandparents are devastated.

"Well, I'm glad they didn't delay their plans to travel. But my grandmother has been complaining my grandfather keeps calling the office. I suppose he's still getting used to the idea that an O'Reilly isn't running the company." With Stephanie out of the picture and James deciding to run the clinic full-time, his grandfather had promoted one of their trusted vice presidents within the company to the position of CEO.

"The O'Reillys still own Medlink. That will have to be enough for now."

"My grandfather's holding out hope for the next generation." James squeezed her hand again. Contentedness whispered across her consciousness and settled in her heart.

"Thank goodness Frank was only bluffing when he claimed to have the files on Regen. He was trying to manipulate Talia into silence and blackmail Stephanie." Lily crossed her arms and drew her shoulders up to her ears. "I don't even want to imagine what would have happened if my research had been compromised."

A soccer ball whizzed by and crashed into his ankles. He bent and picked up the ball when Chloe yelled, "No hands, Daddy."

He dropped the ball and kicked it toward their daughter. "I'm so happy Chloe's adjusted so well. She's been through a lot for a little kid."

"You're a great father. Mrs. Benson knew

what she was doing when she asked you to make sure her granddaughter had a good home." Lily thought her heart would explode as she watched James track the movements of his daughter, the love for her apparent on his face.

He wrapped his arm around Lily's waist and pulled her closer. "You're a great mom."

"Something I never thought I'd be."

"Hey." He ran his knuckle down her cheek, his voice deep and soothing. "We're going to have more children. We're going to fill this yard with little O'Reillys."

"I never thought I'd be a mom or a wife. You made me realize there was more to life than work." Lily tilted her face into his touch. "I can't believe Regen is now showing signs of actually *curing* patients."

God is good.

"Maybe someday we'll be ready to have another child." He placed his hand on her stomach. "Or maybe we'll adopt again. Or both."

Lily playfully tapped James's arm. "How many children do you plan on having?"

James laughed. "As many as God blesses us with. I trust in His plan."

Lily placed her hands on his cheeks and pressed a kiss to his lips. "I trust Him, too."

Lily brushed her hand across James's hair, grown a little longer now that he was officially retired from the army. He was content to stay in Orchard Gardens and run the clinic full-time now that his grandparents had stopped pressuring him to become CEO of Medlink.

She stared into his brown eyes, and the thought of having children with him swirled in her mind. Part him. Part her.

Or another beautiful child just like Chloe would be a blessing.

Lily's gaze drifted to her daughter running around in the yard with her green galoshes on. Her daughter. Yes, God had brought Chloe into their lives for a reason.

Cupping her face in his warm hands, James kissed her back. Tears filled her eyes. Her daughter squealed, and they broke the kiss and both stood staring at her.

"Look at me. I can push the swing, too." Chloe smiled brightly.

"Yes, you can." James scooped up Chloe to delighted squeals. Lily's heart filled with joy as the warm spring sun shined down on her family.

A new beginning...

* * * * *

Dear Reader,

The idea for *Critical Diagnosis* has been bouncing around in my head for a long time. My first job after graduating from Georgia Tech was working as a quality engineer for a large pharmaceutical company. I worked in packaging and had to do everything from checking the torque on a childproof cap (we've all experienced the cap that just wouldn't come off, right?) to ensuring the lot number and expiration date were correct on the label. My job was necessary, but a tad boring. I often envied the researchers, believing their jobs were much more glamorous and certainly more important.

I didn't work long at the pharmaceutical company before marriage relocated me back to Buffalo. After a few different engineering jobs, I left corporate America for full-time motherhood. Eventually, I discovered writing.

Now I get to live vicariously through my heroines in my stories. Not surprisingly, the heroine of *Critical Diagnosis* is Dr. Lily McAllister, a researcher who has devoted her life to finding a cure for the disease that killed her mother and now afflicts her niece—all while being stalked by a killer.

A few early readers of *Critical Diagno-*

sis asked me to name the disease Lily was researching. I purposely didn't name the disease for fear the reader wouldn't believe my heroine had found a treatment or cure for a real disease that currently didn't have many treatment options. Instead, I referred to the fictional disease as a rare, genetic orphan disease. The term *orphan disease* stems from the reluctance of some pharmaceutical companies to support research for a disease with a limited population because there is "no money in it." Sad, but true. (Through my research, I read that more pharmaceutical companies are starting to invest in research for rare diseases due, in part, to patient advocacy, legislation and medical breakthroughs. All great news!) So, if you're scratching your head wondering what disease Lily cured, it has no name. But rest assured, Lily and her family have a bright future.

I hope you enjoyed *Critical Diagnosis*. I love to hear from my readers. Feel free to send me a note at alison@alisonstone.com.

Live, Love, Laugh,

Alison Stone

Questions for Discussion

1. James is conflicted. His grandfather expects him to return to the fold and become CEO of Medlink Pharmaceutical. However, James, a physician, has his heart in practicing medicine. In this case, do you think James is right to follow his heart or do you think he has an obligation to step in and run the company so his ailing grandfather can retire?

2. Lily has spent years doing research to find a cure for the disease that killed her mother and now afflicts her niece. It's not often someone is in a position to make tremendous strides in finding a cure for a disease that hits so close to home. In what other ways can a family member help someone who is battling a life-threatening disease?

3. God loves all His creatures. However, Lily uses lab rats in her research. I learned that these rats are specifically bred for research. Some people feel animal research is necessary to make breakthroughs to help human beings. Other people think research on animals should be avoided at all costs. Others make further distinctions. They find lab rats are okay, but primates are unaccept-

able. How do you feel about this controversial topic?

4. In the course of the story, we learn James's grandparents had disowned their daughter years ago for having a child outside of marriage. Do you believe tough love is acceptable? Or should the grandparents have been more compassionate?

5. Lily learns she, too, carries the gene for the disease that killed her mother. As a result, she is afraid to have children in case she passes the gene on to them. Do you think science and the ability to plan accordingly are good things? Or do you think people need to have more faith in God's plan?

6. Gambling debt plays a role in this story. Some say gambling subscribes to a get-rich-quick appeal, which undermines a person's work ethic. Do you feel this to be true or can gambling be a fun form of entertainment if done in moderation?

7. In some cases, gambling becomes a strong addiction that overtakes a person's life and finances. Discuss other potential reasons gambling can be destructive.

8. Lily's lab assistant Talia has low self-esteem, allowing the "bad guy" to manipulate her. How can we teach young people to have confidence in themselves so they become leaders and not followers?

9. Talia had her plans derailed when she didn't get into the Ph.D. program. Have you ever had to give up a dream? What other doors opened for you?

10. A rash act born of jealousy sets some key events in motion. Why do you think some people are more prone to jealousy than others? Do you think it's a matter of trusting in God's abundance?

11. James spent time in war-torn countries serving as an army physician. What do you think drives people to perform such selfless acts? Would you be able to put aside your fear to do the same thing?

12. Lily continued to pursue her research while her life was at stake. Have you ever pursued a just cause in the face of opposition?

13. Growing up, James was heavily influenced by his wealthy grandparents yet he decided to run a free health-care clinic. How

can we influence young people to lead a life of service to others?

14. Lily and James received their happily-ever-after. That's one of the reasons readers read romance novels. They have the promise of a happy ending. Why do you read them? *Critical Diagnosis* also has a suspense element. Why are you drawn to romantic-suspense novels?

15. Were you surprised to learn James, Lily and Chloe became an instant family?